I0621452

THE LOSER IN THE STATIC

A NOVEL

THOM YOUNG

The Loser in the Static

Copyright © 2020 Thom Young
All rights reserved.

No part of this publication may be reproduced, distributed, or transmitted in any form or by any means, including photocopying, recording, or other electronic or mechanical methods, without the prior written permission of the publisher, except in brief quotations embodied in critical reviews, citations, and literary journals for noncommercial uses permitted by copyright law.

This is a work of fiction. Names, characters, and incidents either are the product of the author's imagination or are used fictitiously, and any resemblance to events, or actual persons—living or dead—is purely coincidental.

No matter how beautiful the outside may be, the inside still has feelings and needs that just words don't fulfill.

—Hubert Selby, Jr.

But what does it mean, the plague? It's life, that's all.

—Albert Camus

Table of Contents

The Loser in the Static

I

I can't say anything about it. I can but you don't want to hear it. Maybe you do but I suppose that depends on both of us. If you're willing to listen, then we can go nowhere fast.

So, it kind of began when I got kicked out of school. I cussed out a teacher. To put it bluntly I told her, "fuck you" and then the principal got pissed and called my parents. Next thing I knew they sent me to see a psychiatrist and everybody thought I was a certified loon. I put on a good act for the shrink and told him all about my problems. Honestly, I don't have any problems except myself. My parents are about as caring and as boring as a kid can hope for. I am not much of a kid. I'm going to be seventeen soon.

I'm in my junior year at a high school in San Antonio. You know when you're supposed to be thinking about college and your future. You know all the crap society expects you to do and the guidance counselors get all giddy about. I don't know what I want to do. I have a hard-enough time being a teenager when it seems some bullied kid walks into school with an assault rifle every other day. The media probably makes it worse than it is and it's not like my friends watch TV. We're on our phones all day, checking our social media feeds or making dumb videos.

Anyways, I have two best friends. Taylor who I've known since first grade. His parents are best friends with my parents. My other friend is Riley. We met freshman year because we had an art class together. Riley likes punk rock like me and we both love playing video games.

I guess by now you should know my name. It's Peyton Pieters. I know it's a crummy name. My last name is spelled wrong. My Dad named me after some football player. I hate football and all sports. A bunch of sweaty guys running around playing grab-ass is not my idea of fun. My last name is from Amsterdam. I'm going there someday. I hear you can get a hooker there and all the drugs you want. It's all legal and there's a bunch of canals that surround the place. I know this because my history teacher, Mr. Anderson, made us do a research project on the origin of our last names. I like Anderson. He isn't a jerk like most teachers.

I'm not very good with girls. There's one girl I tried to put the moves on. She's Amber Wilson. She used to be the head cheerleader and wore short skirts. I can't really think of anything lamer than a pep rally. Most of the students sit in the bleachers and stare at their phones.

Amber graduated last year and went to Baylor. It's in Waco. I read about there being a cult in Waco a long time ago. The government burned them alive because their leader had a bunch of guns. That's not really important to what I'm trying to tell you about Amber. I don't think she knows I exist. I tried to talk to her at a dance but never got the nerve. The only reason I went to the dance was because of her. I felt shitty after nothing happened. I heard she got pregnant by some guy her first semester. Kids are always spreading rumors, so you never know. The real reason I like Amber is because she's a redhead. I have a thing for them. Maybe I'm a little crazy, but I heard Amber is coming home for Christmas break. If I get some balls, I might drop by her house. She lives a few blocks over by the golf course. I probably won't do it because I'm socially awkward. The shrink told me that, but he gets paid to shoot the shit.

My parents said I wouldn't be in school for a while. My Dad mentioned military school so I can get "back on track" whatever that means There wasn't much to do at home. Both my parents work, and they gave me the speech about how it takes two incomes to keep up with the cost of living today. My Dad makes good money by taking other people's money and trying to make them more money. It's all about money. If you get a good education and work hard enough, you can be a big ass winner. It's the great American lie and every year the school tells us the same crap all over again.

I convinced Taylor and Riley to ditch school one day. We did the usual which meant hanging out in the parking lot at All-Sups. We did this pretty much every day after school. It's a good way to pass the time and talk about all the girls at school. I smoke Lucky Strikes, but Riley and Taylor like to vape. I never got into it because if you're going to smoke, you might as well smoke real tobacco. Sometimes there would be a fight if some of the other guys from school showed up.

Most of them are dicks anyways. The ones that get their ass kicked are the ones that mess with me. I have a reputation you know. Riley said kids had been talking at school and that several girls we're crazy over me because they think I'm a rebel. I don't understand what being a rebel is anyways. It seems like the only time you're a rebel is when somebody else wants you to do something against the rules and to me that's a crock of shit. I guess I should be telling you about the part where I had to go to reform school.

It started when my Dad took my smartphone. My Mom and him had already packed up all my stuff and put it in the back of the station wagon. I think my family is the only one that still drives a station wagon. It probably has something to do with my Dad being a real nerd. He's a pretty good guy, I mean, if you must have a father, he's a good one. The thing that bothered me was that they didn't tell me. I was going away to this horrible place. St. Mark's Academy. A school for boys with a future. I didn't say goodbye when they dropped me off. I gave my Mom a hug and winked at my Dad to say it didn't bother me all that much. I watched them drive away. I decided to make the best of it.

St. Mark's Academy has been around since the nineteenth century. In case you're wondering, that's the century the Civil War was fought in. Their mission is to give boys a future, in other words they are going to break you. After they do that, you have no choice but to submit to their tradition of hypocrisy and cruelty. Then after that, your parents will be proud about your future again. Maybe they are wrong for thinking we want a future in the first place. In fact, they might be the reason we don't care about the future. The older generations ruined everything, and they expect us to be excited about it. I don't feel like playing the game.

They give you a roommate at St Mark's right away. I ended up with this big guy, Larry, who had pimples all over his face. Larry said he was from Ohio and that his father was a big shot in the military. Larry liked to talk all the time and after a while I stopped listening. I'm not sure how Larry ended up here, but I got a hunch he was going to ruin my life. Despite his obvious bad characteristics, Larry was a guy you didn't mind having around too much. He's a goon that thinks you really are his friend. Larry would probably kick anybody's ass because he thought you were his friend. I knew this might come in handy at Ol' St. Mark's. There are all kinds of creeps here that like to steal and do bad things. I needed Larry to watch my back. I might be a bad person, but I know how to use other bad people to my advantage.

After about a week, I figured out how things work at St. Mark's and already planned an escape. They don't let you bring cell phones inside St. Mark's, but this one kid Jason Andrews somehow got his iPhone inside. He may have stuck it up his ass. I borrowed his phone one night, and I knew it was stupid, but I texted Riley and Taylor and told them about my plans. I figure if your friends can't keep their traps shut then they're not your friends. All you must do is follow orders and keep your neck clean.

I hadn't met any of the other guys besides Larry. There's one guy in my history class named Rex. He seemed cool and told me he was into skating. I have like twenty skateboards at home. I'm the best skater you've ever seen. I told Rex we should skip class and go skate. He said he would think about it. If we got caught, it would mean more time at St. Mark's. I decided to go it alone and take my chances. I needed to spend time alone and hit the road. I read a book by Kerouac about living life and being free while travelling. I like the book a lot. Same with Camus. He was this guy who was depressed all the time and lived in France. He was one of the first existentialists. Basically, they were a group of artists and writers that sat around and talked about how everything is pointless. I kind of see why I like him.

The night I left was uneventful. I simply strolled out under the cover of darkness and slid through the fence. I got everything in my backpack. I didn't know how to function without my phone. You don't know how you are until you don't have it. It's when you're at your lowest that you find the strength. When there's nothing left to lose that's when you become a loser. I patted my pockets often, feeling that buzz you expect every waking moment, but it still wasn't there.

So, my adventure started at a gas station. I had enough money to hop a bus to Dallas. I felt like I was living in the seventies or something. The guy gave me a nervous look. I asked him something he probably hadn't heard in a long time, and that was if he had a phone book. He said no, so I asked him if there was a bus station close by and he said there was one five blocks up on the corner of Smith and Western. I thanked him, which I rarely do because I'm kind of a bad guy. I mean if people are nice to me then I'm nice in return. I find that most people aren't nice, especially when they get older. I suppose getting old is kind of shitty.

I found the bus station and sat there for about an hour until the bus came. It was cold as hell and I didn't have my jacket. So, what I did was kind of hug myself. I must have looked insane. I didn't have a ticket, but I handed the driver a twenty, which I wanted to use for food later. He said that wasn't enough. But in that moment, I guess he felt sorry for my crazy-looking self and nodded his head towards the back with a thin smile. I made my way to the back of the bus. The bus was crowded and smelt like shit. There were all kinds of people looking miserable and everything. I sat down in the back seat and put my cap on. I tried to sleep but knew it was pointless.

I'll make this part short and tell you that the entire trip was hell. I try not to say hell too much on account of my folks being religious. I believe in God but sometimes I'm not sure. I don't understand how God can treat people so badly. I stared out the window. I looked at the lights and it seemed there was nothing but shopping malls and every now and then you could make out a sign that said Walmart or Costco. Everything looked the same and I was upset about it. I needed a cigarette but there were no smoking signs everywhere. They're always messing everything up. You know when you're younger, you have to put up with a lot less shit than when you get old. Life begins and the next thing you know you're an adult and you have four kids and a mortgage and it's over.

It was morning when I got to Dallas and the bus dropped me off downtown. I needed to eat and get coffee. I thought about Riley and Taylor and if they were keeping their mouths shut. I knew St. Mark's would tell my parents soon and they'd send out the SWAT team or something. Don't think they'd waste the taxpayer money on some deadbeat kid like me. Not like I was a real danger, just surviving.

I know my Grandmother is too old to care that I'm in Dallas. In fact, her house isn't too far in the old neighborhood of Highland Park. Another place full of rich bastards and a bunch of spoiled brats that get everything they want. I'm pretty much like them. I suppose you kind of take it for granted when you get nice stuff all the time.

I walked a few blocks and found this little restaurant that served breakfast. I ordered some scrambled eggs and a side of bacon. I like scrambled eggs over fried eggs because my Grandfather always liked fried eggs and my Grandfather was a rich bastard. He died a few years ago and he was buried in this big cemetery called Rest Haven. Everybody got all sad at his funeral but my Dad. From what I've heard, my Dad's childhood pretty much sucked. I mean my Grandfather beat his ass all the time and maybe he deserved it. I don't think it's right to beat your kids.

I finished breakfast and sat there staring off into space. I thought about Amber but figured she didn't care about me. I don't trust people that much, especially women. I kind of look old for my age, so I figured if I hung around long enough, I might meet a classy lady like you see in those old movies. Everything seems real in the movies. You can see yourself in them and pretend you have a better life. I left the diner and started walking until I found a bar. A lot of the time they don't card me. I suppose it's an advantage but there's a lot of assholes that card everybody. I mean they card everyone, even creepy old guys that look like they're sixty-five. That's what's wrong with society, nobody has any goddamn common sense. My Grandfather used to say that all the time. It doesn't matter now because he's dead.

I left another ten and waited for the server to go into the kitchen and just left. The bar is named, The Landing. It used to cater to real alcoholics back in the day but now all these damn hipsters hang out here. I walked up to the bar and tried to order a beer. The bartender didn't even give it a second thought and handed me a cold one. I took a seat at the counter and drank it down. It felt good to be alone and have a drink. Sometimes all you need in life is to get drunk. Being drunk is better than being sober. I couldn't make up my mind about what to do next. I know a hotel downtown that's kind of classy. I had a few more beers and then made my way down there. It's rumored that they have a lot of high-class prostitutes that work in the lobby. I'm still a virgin and everything, but I have made out with a few chicks. It sounds bad, but I made out with Melissa Reeves at a youth group weekend. I might go to hell for that one. Anyways, Melissa is kind of known as the school slut. I think every football player has banged her.

I had five more beers and I was feeling rather good. I was almost drunk. I have a high tolerance. I paid my tab and then I walked back outside. I headed down to the hotel to see if any action was going on. For some reason, I was thinking about Amber. She has spell on me. You know girls can do that, as they smile and break your heart. I made it to the hotel and walked up to the lobby bar. There were a couple of business types sitting there in their suits. I just knew that they screwed people all the time. They probably took their money and didn't feel bad about it at all. I ordered a martini with a green olive. I sat there and felt rather good for some time, until it got crowded.

I stumbled back into the lobby to see if there were some whores. One girl looked fine. She had on a tight black dress that hugged her ass. I liked her right away. I noticed she was kind of checking me out, but you never can tell with women. The alcohol made me feel a little brave, so I walked over to her. I was putting the old charm on her. I told her that I was in town for business and that I had a room, but I was about to check out. I didn't think she was a prostitute but she kind of hinted that she might want some money. I told her I had some dough and that we could maybe talk later. She said that sounded good and took a seat. We sat down in the lobby and she told me about how she used to live in Mexico. Her dad is some bigwig oil guy. She said her father made everybody move there when she was a kid. I thought she looked like she was twenty-five. I started to get a little bored but then she suggested we head up to her room. I almost hesitated, but being drunk, I agreed.

I followed her up to the room. She had a bottle of wine in the mini fridge. I poured two glasses and tried to look sophisticated. She sat on the bed and crossed her legs. I didn't know her name. I sat next to her. I wasn't sure what to do. Then she leaned over and kissed me. I thought I was going to make it but then she pulled away from me and started talking about money, which I imagined was going to be a lot. I told her I didn't think she was a prostitute. She laughed and then it was over. I wished her the best and walked out of the room. There was nothing else to do so I went back to the bar and drank. I blacked out and the next thing I knew I was at McDonald's eating a cheeseburger. I was alone again. I thought about my parents and how worried they probably were by now. I didn't care all that much. This was a life worth living.

I took a taxi and rode around. I finally told the driver to take me to this little Mexican restaurant. I could have a few margaritas and eat some enchiladas. I remembered that Riley and I came up to Dallas one time and ate here. My Dad had business and he took us. If I remember correctly, there wasn't much to do besides stay at the hotel and Riley flushed a cherry bomb down the toilet. We both could have done jail time for that prank. Luckily, nobody found out and we both went back to San Antonio laughing our asses off. You should have heard Riley tell it to the other kids at school. He made it sound like he set a grenade off. I ordered a plate of fajitas as well as cheese enchiladas. I was full after that and then I walked back outside. I didn't know where I was going.

That's how I feel about life. It's like everybody expects you to do something with your life but nobody considers that maybe you don't want to do anything. I think it's ingrained inside humans to want to do things. I think our society values hard work. I hate work.

I decided to walk back to the bus station. I didn't even know what time it was, just steady darkness. I thought my parents were probably losing their shit by now. Maybe freezing my ass off on the bus for a few hours would do me some good. I need direction but then again, I really don't care. I sat there for a while, not hugging my body again since I was warm all over. The bus finally came by and I gave him enough money to make his eyebrows raise. He didn't give me change. People are always looking to rip you off.

I sat in the back of the bus again and we started rolling down the interstate. We headed south. The thing about living in San Antonio is that everybody knows it for the Alamo. I've been there so many times it seems like some kind of amusement park. A place to get cotton candy and get all mushy about history and everything. The worst were the field trips. It seems we always went to the Alamo on field trips. There's nothing else to see besides the Alamo in San Antonio. I don't believe the official story. They probably were just a bunch of guys that wanted to get drunk and a war broke out. I think you know the rest of the story. Mexico kicked everybody's ass and then after that Texas kicked Mexico's ass. That's pretty much how we won our independence. I've read about it in history books for most of my life. Besides, my Dad told me the story when I was still taking craps in my diapers. I went to sleep.

When I woke up, we were in San Antonio and the bus driver was yelling at me to get off. I was still a fairly good way from home. I live in an area called Alamo Heights. It's where the rich people live. I never saw us as being rich, but I guess we have more money than most people. I started walking home.

Sometimes, we would hitchhike around the city and see if we could get drunk on Friday nights. Riley and I usually got drunk while Taylor got all the girls. He's a lady's man and always seems to get the prettiest ones. If I get lucky sometimes, I get the girls that are a bit thicker. They need love as much as everybody else and sometimes I admit they're pretty fun. I still get made fun of because I haven't been laid. It's like I'm saving myself for somebody special. I knew if I had the chance, I would go all the way with Amber. She seems like the one to me.

I stuck my thumb out and this truck pulled over and I hopped inside. I gave him my address and he took me right to my front door. You should have seen the look on my parents' faces when they saw me. My Mom hugged me, and my Dad almost cried. I knew I was going to be in a lot of trouble, but nothing really happened. I told them how miserable I was at St. Mark's. They said that I should probably get some counseling. I knew it was just another way of them trying to fix something that didn't need to be fixed. I have some problems but probably not any more than any other kid.

My birthday was in a few weeks and I would be seventeen. That's legal age in Texas. I only had one more year to graduate. I know my dad wants me to go to the University of Texas. I really hate Austin. The traffic sucks and there's too many people. San Antonio is bigger than Austin. I live in a bubble though. I mean Alamo Heights is kind of its own little world. None of the moms work except mine. I guess my Mom kind of feels like she must maintain an image. That there's value in working hard. I told you about all those things.

My Dad mentioned that Saint Mark's was pissed off about me leaving. I thought about it but realized since they already had my Dad's money, it didn't matter. I remembered that it was Christmas break.

**

It was unusually cold in San Antonio that winter. I messed around with Riley and Taylor and got drunk a couple of times. I heard that Amber wasn't pregnant at all. It turned out some dumbass made it up. She didn't even have a boyfriend. There were a couple of days left of the break so one night I decided to walk over to Amber's house. I walked up to the door and knocked. I know her folks because my parents play tennis with them at the Country Club. I think Amber knows I like her. I stood outside her door. To my surprise, Amber opened the door and smiled. She looked like an angel and I felt my heartbeat increase. She asked how I was doing and that she had heard that I had been sent away to reform school. I asked her how things were at Baylor and if she was enjoying her classes. It seemed like we stood in the doorway forever.

Finally, I told her that I should get going but to my surprise, she reached out and hugged me. I felt her nice breasts press up against my chest. I tried to catch my breath but then realized I looked like a big dork. I told her bye and walked back home. We said we would try to see each other again.

My Dad worked out a deal with the principal and I got to go back to school. I was on my last chance. If I messed up again, then I was done. I had to admit that it felt good being back. It was kind of fun to see everybody and it seemed that I turned into a legend. I noticed a lot of the girls were coming around. Maybe getting into all that trouble wasn't so bad after all. I needed something good to happen because sometimes life screws you over.

Riley mentioned that this kid Jason Winters was throwing a big party. Everybody was bringing beer and dates and some other kid mentioned he might bring some weed. I don't like weed. I would much rather have a beer or vodka seven. None of the kids could shut up about the party so I knew it was going to be lame. Amber was supposed to be there, too. It was probably worth checking out just because of that. Riley and I planned on getting drunk before the party. There's nothing like getting wasted before you start partying.

Riley and I went to the party already hammered. Taylor said he didn't care about going so he stayed home and got drunk by himself. Riley and I would probably head over to Taylor's if the party got lame. It seemed like every kid from school was there. I stood around and looked for Amber, but I didn't see her. Riley disappeared with this girl that we knew from the art class. I grabbed a beer and walked outside by the patio. There was a swimming pool and some kids were hanging out and drinking. Then I saw her. Amber was sitting down under a tree and it looked like she was crying. I walked over to her and said hello. She seemed kind of excited to see me. I asked her if she was sad and she said she wasn't. I knew she was lying.

Then she mentioned something about a boy she met up at Baylor. She told me things didn't work out and that she was feeling kind of down about it. I asked if she wanted to go and she did. I figured that Riley would be rather good without me anyways. Amber and I walked in the street and started heading in the direction of her house. I think she knew I was drunk. I put my arm around her, and she didn't pull away. I walked her home and to my surprise, she laid a big wet kiss on me. I saw stars. She said she would try to visit before she went back to Baylor.

**

The next thing you knew I was a senior. I tried to stay on the straight and narrow. My grades were rather good, and I even applied to attend Texas Tech in Lubbock. Amber and I were keeping in touch. She sent me a text sometimes. I didn't forget about that kiss. I wanted to see her again but she's dating a football player. That's the way it always seems. When you finally get the girl, she walks away.

It's always the man that has true feelings. Women can leave you and not feel bad about it. One day you're making out and the next she's on a train somewhere with another guy. You needn't worry about these things too much because she's probably already got another stooge waiting in the wings.

I should probably tell you about my brother. His name was Sam, but he died when I was only ten years old. I don't think my parents will ever get over it. After he was buried my Mother shut the door to his room. He was a real athlete and had a full scholarship to play at SMU. I go in there sometimes. I look at all his trophies and pictures he got for his accomplishments. I think my Mom and Dad are afraid to go into his room.

Anyways, he was killed by a drunk driver. You think that would have stopped me from drinking, but it made me want to drink more. So, I went in there and sat on his bed. I started thinking about when we were younger and how much I looked up to him. Maybe that's why I am so messed up now. If Sam didn't die, I would be a lot happier. So, going to his room is a special place for me. I can gather my thoughts and think about him. Everybody loved Sam because he was such a nice guy. I never heard anybody say one bad thing about him. I feel like a disappointment compared to Sam.

I know my parents probably feel the same, but they never talk about it. My Dad gives me this look and then my Mom shakes her head. I know they love me but sometimes I'm not sure. I mean that sounds stupid, but maybe it would be better if I had never been born. I can never live up to my older brother. I wish I died in that car wreck. I wonder why God always takes the best people and leaves the screw-ups.

Everybody at school is excited about the homecoming game and dance. I didn't even go last year. There aren't even any girls I'm interested in. I think about Amber every day, but she probably doesn't give a damn. Most of the time, I go to bed early and feel sorry for myself. It's a crummy existence. The teachers even started calling my folks and telling them I was slipping up. They said I seem down on myself and I suppose they're right. My mind isn't on schoolwork or the future at all. A counselor at school has some concerns about me and called my Mom. Honestly, I don't want to help myself. I feel like my heart has a big hole in it.

On the night of the game, I didn't go to the stadium. I stood on a hill and looked down on everything. I felt stupid. I could see all the cheerleaders getting excited and the crowd going crazy. I didn't even know who was winning the game and to be honest, I didn't care. Riley and Taylor both had dates and they kept talking about how they were going to get lucky. I felt like I was in a weird dream. It's like I could see everything that was going on, but I wasn't there. My mind was somewhere else. I felt Amber haunting everything inside of me. I shouldn't be hung up on a girl like this much. Your feelings get confused and you don't know what to do. I've never been in love, but I think this is the closest thing to it. What's funny is that I haven't seen her in a long time. It's stupid to think somebody cares about you when they don't. That's usually how everything is, one person cares and the other person doesn't. After the game, I walked home. My parents went out to eat so I had the house to myself. I went into Sam's room and opened the window. I took out my cigarettes and lit one up. I looked down into the backyard and could see the shadows playing along the fence. The swimming pool is empty this year. I always feel better alone.

The only thing better would have been to have Amber there. I smoked a while and then shut the window. I went back downstairs and sat on the couch. I turned on the television and there was this old black and white cowboy movie on. Most of them have the same plot. Some bad guy rides into town with a black hat and then the good guy comes with the white hat on. The good guy always wins and rides away with the girl and then that's how it ends.

I wish it was the other way around. I would love to see the bad guy come into town and kill everybody. After that, he would get drunk and then shoot up everybody else in the next town. You never see movies like that. If I directed movies the bad guy would always win. To me, that's more interesting and besides who likes watching some movie where the good guy wins? That's not how life works. Most of the time the bad guys win and it's hard to tell who's bad or good.

I got bored of watching TV so then I went outside and started throwing rocks. That's what I do when I get bored. I find as many rocks as I can and then I throw them. I'm not trying to hit anything. I like throwing them for no reason. After that, I went back inside and went to sleep. I don't know what I'm going to do tomorrow but it's probably going to involve getting drunk. Another thing I do when I'm drunk is sometimes I cut myself. Other times I get a cigarette and burn it on my hand. It leaves these little red circles that look like ant bites. My mom always asks me what happened, and I tell her that I fell skating. I think it's alright to lie sometimes. If you're lying and it works out for the best, then it's okay.

2

About a week later, my Grandfather on my Mom's side died. Sometimes nothing makes sense. It's like society expects you to be somebody that you don't want to be. I had a semester left and I couldn't figure things out. All the popular kids have everything planned. They are going to some fancy college or staying home for a while and working. My Dad isn't happy with my decision. I know he has always wanted me to go to the University of Texas at Austin. The thought of living in Austin is too much. I think it was cool back in the seventies.

The only thing I know about it back then is from what I've seen on TV or in some old magazines with Willie Nelson and Waylon Jennings. If I do go to Tech, I will make a trip out to Littlefield. That's the home of my favorite country singer Waylon Jennings. If you don't know much about him, he was a real outlaw. I think he had like nine wives and snorted cocaine all day. I'm pretty sure he and Willie could have put any rockstar to shame back in the day. I think today all the music sucks. I mean Riley and Taylor listen to depressing emo music. I feel that way all the time, so I don't need some band to tell me about it.

I have these strange dreams and wake up sweating. I don't know why I have them, but they are sometimes pretty violent. I dreamt I walked into school with an assault rifle and killed everybody I can see. Although I would never do anything like that, it scares me. Of course, I will never admit that I care about people. I tell my Mom and Dad I love them, but it's hard for me to express how I feel. I want to tell Amber how I feel about her.

I should tell you what happened for the rest of my senior year. Riley got busted with weed and got suspended for a week. Taylor and I would meet him at All-Sup's and smoke cigarettes and talk about our futures. One of the things Riley and I would say is "fuck the future". I'm a real creep and only care about the now. I think life should be that way and that you should enjoy the moment. All of society is so worried about what's going to happen in the future, that they miss out on life. They waste their lives thinking about something that hasn't happened.

**

The next thing I knew we only had a couple of weeks until graduation. There is this kid, James. He is kind of like a ghost in school and everybody avoids him like the plague. I talked to the guy a couple of times and I tried to be nice. I relate to those that are outcasts. What's bad is a lot of the jocks are bullying him. I remember one day this kid told me that James had been talking about shooting up the school. Nobody took it seriously.

One day I was in my biology class and they said that we were on lockdown. It's sad but that's kind of the norm for most schools nowadays. It seems like every other week there's a school shooting. The strange thing is that you never really worry about it until it affects you. Most people don't give a shit unless it affects them. They don't care that kids are dying in Africa or there are all kinds of homeless people. They only care about themselves and to be honest it's shitty.

I didn't tell you what happened with that kid, James. It turns out that he didn't have a big gun and there wasn't a shooting. He had a BB gun in his backpack, and it freaked everyone out. I think he's a messed-up kid, but I know it's only a matter of time before he does kill a lot of people. I can see how it happens. You get bullied enough and treated like crap, then you want to take out some revenge on all the assholes.

**

I had a week off before graduation so Riley, Taylor, and I decided to take a little trip to Mexico. We went to a resort my parents always go to when they want to get away from their jobs and boring lives. Some other kids went too, and our parents trusted us because this kid Maxwell's parents were supposed to chaperone everybody.

"Did you bring the weed?" Taylor asked.

"I know a guy here that can get us some high-quality shit," Riley replied.

"You think you wouldn't touch that shit after getting suspended," I said.

We had just gotten to the resort and already my friends were talking about smoking weed. Luckily for Riley, his dad is a lawyer and got him out of his situation. Now, my two best friends will be walking the stage with me. Then we will throw our caps up in the air and celebrate all the shit that's going to be in our future. Riley is even talking about marrying his girlfriend that he met a couple of months ago. I don't know if I can think of anything dumber than marrying a girl you just met. At our age, you're too damn young to fall in love.

I must sound like a hypocrite because I am in love with Amber. I think about her all the time. I've even thought about driving up to Waco and seeing if I can find her. My parents said that she's coming home for the summer. I think if she does, I will head over to her house. I will feel like a big dork and probably piss myself. When you think about it, it's really stupid to be in love. It doesn't work out and you get a broken heart and then some girl is always on your mind. Love is the biggest lie of all time. You find someone that you get along with and you stay with them. You never really know if you're in love because nobody knows what love is and it's a crock of shit.

I'd like to tell you that we had a great time at the resort, but I rarely saw Riley or Taylor. They were too busy chasing some girls. That kid, Maxwell, got drunk and puked in the pool. That was the highlight of the trip and then we went home. We were going to graduate. Our lives could now get on the right track as my Dad said before I went to that shitty reform school.

I wonder how all the bastards are up at St. Mark's. You talk about a bunch of hypocrites, there's nothing worse than a bunch of guys acting like they love God but at the same time beating the shit out of you. I mean that's what they did in the Old Testament. God would tell all the people in Israel to go into these villages and kill everyone. Then everybody would have a party and start worshipping other gods and get drunk. Then God would get mad and start kicking the shit out of everyone. The people would feel bad and then they would start following God again. Then God would tell them to go into some other village and kill everybody again. I like the Old Testament better than the New Testament. Don't get me wrong, the New Testament is pretty cool. I think Jesus is a great guy, and if there is a Jesus, he's probably up in heaven laughing his ass off. It's almost like his father played a trick on everybody and created humans.

If Adam stood up to Eve in the Garden of Eden, we wouldn't have all these problems today. I suppose he was the first man that was pussy-whipped. Ever since then, it's been nothing but trouble. I feel this way about Amber. I've said it before, but she has a hold on me. Girls are witches that have this strange power. Once they get in your head they never leave. Even when you meet a new girl you still think about the old one. It's an endless cycle of being in love or thinking you're in love. You spend your life trying to find something that doesn't exist. God has been lying to us since the beginning of time.

I should tell you about when I was a kid. I was born in San Antonio and grew up in a house by this park. I would go there and start digging around in ant mounds. I liked burning all the ants with a magnifying glass. My parents didn't care that I was gone all day. I guess they wanted me out of the house. I remember one day I saw something bad. I didn't understand it but there was this old guy and he was peeking up the skirts of the girls on the swing set. I mean he was really a pervert. Old people are always doing things like that. The girls were just trying to have some fun at the park and here's this creepy old pervert. I'll never forget that day. I feel like I lost something. It may have been my innocence but that's when I realized that being an adult sucks.

I never thought I would grow up. There really isn't much to say. I grew up in a great family. I have everything I ever wanted. I get new video games every Christmas and my Grandmas always give me money. I'm like any other kid. My parents have more money than most, but it doesn't matter. When you get older you realize everything is about money. You must get a job and earn it. Everybody wants to have more of it. And the more you have the more miserable you are. If you don't have enough, you're better off not knowing about it. I'm not sure if you're born an idiot or become an idiot because of all the dumb things you do. It's better if you don't realize it. There's excitement in not knowing how dumb you are. They say ignorance is bliss.

**

There were two days before graduation, and everybody decided to get drunk at Riley's house. There were a bunch of girls and all the guys were getting all mushy about them. I didn't feel like doing anything. My mind was on Amber. I walked outside and started throwing rocks. I already told you this is what I like to do when my mind is clouded up.

Everybody is all excited about graduation but me. Both my Grandmothers sent me checks for about five grand combined. That's a lot of dough. I'm supposed to use it for spending money up at Tech. I forgot to tell you I got accepted there. I don't give a damn about college. So, what I did was sneak out one night. I took a bus up to Waco. I was going to miss graduation. Besides, the whole thing is a dog and pony show. Everybody gets all excited because you're entering the next stage in life. All the teachers and parents cream themselves on how they helped you be successful. After that, nobody cares what you do.

I get these obsessions in my mind and I must go through with them. I cashed the checks, so I had plenty of money. I didn't know when I would be back home and to be honest, I didn't care. I brought my phone so I could still check in with Riley and Taylor. They were probably pissed about me not walking with them, but they'd come around. I realized after Sam's death that life is too short to not do what you want.

So, I sat in the back of the bus and started thinking. I didn't want to go to Tech. It would mean more classes that I didn't want to take and meeting people I didn't care about. I started fumbling with my cigarettes in my coat pocket. I needed one but realized I couldn't smoke on the bus. I went to Waco because of Amber.

**

When I got to Waco, the bus dropped me off close to campus. I took out my phone and texted Amber. I never heard back. It started getting dark, so I needed to find a place to stay for the night. There are a bunch of bars on Sixth Street. The only hotel in the area sits right on the interstate but you can walk to the bars. I checked into the hotel and then I decided to get drunk.

I walked a few blocks and then I saw this bar that didn't look crowded. I walked up to the bar and tried to order a beer, but the bartender carded me. I pulled out my fake ID and I got a cold one. I felt suave sitting at the bar. I planned to try and get a hold of Amber the next day. I kept drinking and the next thing you knew I was with this girl in another bar. I hate dancing but I was on the dance floor and I had my tongue in this girl's mouth. I didn't even know her name. She grabbed me by the hand, and we walked out into the street and there were people everywhere. She started to lead me somewhere but then she just disappeared in the crowd. It was like I didn't learn my lesson. Either way, I got some nachos at this food truck. It helped me sober up and then I went back to the hotel and passed out.

I woke up at about ten the next morning and I was afraid to check my phone. I couldn't resist and I had about twenty messages from my parents and there were a few from Riley. I trusted Riley so I replied to him, but I didn't even think about replying to my parents. I went down to the hotel lobby and had coffee. I wasn't too far from Baylor's campus, so I decided to walk on over there. Baylor has a pretty swanky campus because it's funded by the Southern Baptist Convention. However, a couple of years ago, a bunch of their football players got accused of rape.

Baylor's football team had been atrocious for years but then they started winning every game. I think their head coach turned a blind eye because they were winning. Nobody cared until these allegations came out and now, they are under the NCAA's microscope. Turns out that their coach was fired last year. I told you earlier that I hate sports. The reason that I kind of follow college football is that my Dad likes to watch it on the weekends.

Nothing was going on, so I walked over to the Student Union building and got myself a Coca-

Cola. I try not to drink too many Cokes but sometimes I need a little sugar to calm my nerves. I texted Amber again, but I didn't hear back. I left the Student Union and started walking around campus and I saw this big ass dorm. A student was coming outside so I told him to hold the door. I walked inside and there was this lady behind the counter in the lobby and I asked her if she knew Amber Wilson. She told me that she didn't and asked what I was doing. I told her that Amber is a friend and that I hadn't seen her in a long time. I felt looking for her seemed pointless, so I walked back outside, and this girl was coming towards me and she looked rather good. I introduced myself and I asked her if she happened to know Amber Wilson. To my surprise, she told me that she did. I told her that Amber is a good friend of mine. She told me that Amber lives in another dorm on the other side of campus. I got directions and walked over there.

I felt stupid but I had come this far, so I wasn't going to give up. I hung out outside the dorm and waited for someone to come outside. This one guy finally came, and I asked him to hold the door. I texted Amber again and told her that I was on campus. I figure by now she thinks I'm a psycho. I sat in this plush chair in the lobby and stared at my phone. After about an hour, I still hadn't heard anything. I walked outside and then my phone vibrated. It was a message from Amber. She told me that she wasn't on campus but stayed over at a friend's house. I presumed that she was probably at some guy's house. I started to feel crummy, so I left the campus and went back to the bus station. I had two options at that point. I could take a bus back to San Antonio or head north to Dallas. I decided on the latter. I chain-smoked until the bus came.

**

I didn't feel like staying in Dallas. I planned on taking another bus to Santa Fe, New Mexico. I had been there a couple of times with my folks and I knew the city well. I like their Square and there's always a lot of merchants selling junky type things like old jewelry and Native American blankets. I know an old hotel that's a perfect place to stay for a while.

Before I knew it, I was on the bus headed to Santa Fe. I probably should have stayed in Waco and waited around for Amber. I had come all this way, and I could have waited a little longer. Something told me that she didn't want to see me anyways. The best thing I can do is leave and get her off my mind. I know that's impossible. It doesn't matter because I missed graduation and felt like a loser. My life is stuck somewhere between alive and static.

I never made it to Santa Fe. I told the bus driver to let me off about fifty miles outside Dallas. I had a great big hole in my heart. I'm crazy because I can't shake Amber out of my mind. I laugh mad with the pain. I decided to hitchhike back. I can take another bus back to Waco and then try to find Amber. I like hitchhiking, I do. Some trucker picked me up and it rained like hell back to Dallas. I told him to take me to the bus station downtown. I don't think God likes me because all my cigarettes were wet, and I had nothing to do until my bus came. I felt low. It's probably the worst I've ever felt. That's saying something because I've felt horrible so many times I can't even goddamn count.

"What ya doing here kid?"

At first, I didn't notice the old guy talking to me. I got kind of pissed that he even asked me such a lousy question.

"Just minding my business old man."

"Minding your business?"

"Waiting for the fucking bus and freezing my ass off." I was trying to get rid of the guy.

"Have you ever been to the JFK museum down at Dealey Plaza?"

"Why would I go to a crummy place like that? Besides, that was a long time ago. Nobody gives a rat's ass about Kennedy getting his brains blown out anymore. The government wants us to forget it ever happened."

"I disagree because I was there, and I remember crying. I felt a little better when they arrested Oswald."

"Listen, old man…if you think Oswald shot Kennedy then I'll sell you a bag of rocks."

I could see the anger building up in his eyes. The old man shook his head and gave me a dirty look then he left. I could have been friendly, but I wasn't in the mood. I had too much on my mind with the whole Amber thing. One entertaining thing was I checked Snapchat and saw a couple of pictures of Riley and Taylor at a graduation party.

They looked wasted and I missed out on the fun. It always seems that way. When things are starting to go right, everything goes wrong. I'm not sure why I didn't want to be there. I looked around the bus station and saw a bunch of people that looked miserable like me. Life had disappointed all of us. If I had a gun, I probably would have killed everybody there. Of course, I would never do that. I mean I might do it, but I'd have to have a better reason than feeling down and everything.

The bus finally came. I gave the driver my ticket and then sat in the back row, watching the rain. It seemed appropriate that I feel depressed. I always felt that depression was something some quack made up. Now I know it's not. It's a disease and the sickness never leaves you. I closed my eyes and went to sleep, and I admit it was some of the best sleep that I've had in a long time.

**

I got dropped off at the Baylor campus, again. I found a bench and sat down. I looked at my phone and I had tons of messages from my parents. There were a few from Riley and Taylor too. They said everyone is going crazy trying to find out where I am. I didn't text anybody back, except for Amber. To my surprise, she replied and said that she was at her dorm. It feels like some light is in the darkness of my heart. My hair was dripping wet and I must have looked like a complete fool. I think I have rather good hair. I wear it kind of like Tony Hawk. I have a bunch of old skating magazines from the eighties and that's kind of my style. Anyways, my hair was soaking wet and it was hanging down in my face. I started feeling a little better thinking that I might see Amber.

I walked over to Amber's dorm. She came down and let me inside. I didn't know what to say to her. I was afraid she might think that I'm a complete idiot. Of course, usually, I am an idiot. She looked better than ever and she had on these tight shorts. I smiled and put the old charm on her. She led me up to her room and we sat on the bed. We talked for a little bit and I basically spilled my guts. I know you should never do that with a girl. They like a guy that's a mystery. You probably know this, but women like guys that are assholes. I started telling her that I missed her and how I felt about her. I knew it turned her off. She told me that she was going to meet some friends later. I knew what was coming next. She mentioned her boyfriend. The pain began to ache in my heart again. Then it happened. Amber leaned over and kissed me. She said I was sweet. Sometimes true love isn't all that true. What I mean is one person is in love and the other person isn't. The truth is a beautiful mistake.

I knew things were over with Amber. I never will get over it. It's true what they say about being friends with the one you love. You can't be both. I almost cried which probably looked weak. I told her goodbye and I walked back outside. One is never sure what might happen next. I thought about going home but then I changed my mind. The thought of Amber being with some other guy eats me up. I went back to the bus stop and wanted to die. I was sick of the goddamn bus. Then I thought about a place that I want to go to. It's one of the places you see in those old movies a lot. I can figure things out there and then drop off the face of the planet.

3

The next day, I decided to take a bus down to Austin and then a flight to New York City. I found a pretty cheap flight using my smartphone. Can you imagine having to call a travel agent back in the eighties or the goddamn airline to go anywhere? The past must have sucked. I think we take the technology we have today for granted. We have it too easy. It's made everyone lazy and fat.

I was sitting in the airport looking at all the people from all over the country. I kind of got disgusted looking at all these miserable, out of shape people sitting around. It seems everybody is looking at their phones and completely oblivious to life going on around them. Before you know it, you've completely wasted your life looking at a glowing screen. Of course, my generation doesn't know any different. We grew up with information overload at our fingertips. No wonder kids are killing other kids all the time. Their parents completely ignore them.

The first thing I did before getting on the plane was buy a goddamn coat. I wasn't going to freeze my ass off in New York. Luckily, my flight wasn't very crowded. This fat bastard came and sat right by me. That's how things always seem in life. Once we got up in the air, I moved to another seat. I like sitting by the window. For a few hours, you are above all the shit on the ground. All the buildings and people look like ants. Then eventually you can't see anything but the clouds. I felt better and I wasn't thinking about Amber. I closed my eyes and tried to go to sleep. It seemed as soon as we got up in the air the pilot said that we were getting ready to land. I must have dozed off and the fact that no bastard was sitting next to me helped.

I've never been to New York City. I probably should have taken the subway, but I decided to take a taxi. I told the driver that I wanted to go see the Statue of Liberty. That Sinatra song where he sings, "If you can make it here you can make it anywhere", never mentions how the mob backed his every move. No wonder that drunk bastard made it. I mentioned that I'm not a fan of history, but I love the mafia. I have watched the goddamn Godfather fifty times. The Godfather Part 2 is my favorite. It's one of the few sequels that is better than the original. The only other movie that's better than the original is Jaws 2. The only sad part is that Jaws didn't eat all those dumb kids that were out sailing. The ending sucks too where Jaws bites into that big ass electric cable and gets fried. If I directed the movie Jaws would have killed everyone.

The people in Texas are friendly. It's a fact that Texas means friendship. I hear the people in New York City are rude. I don't know about that, but people are rude no matter where you go. My taxi driver didn't seem thrilled with me getting in his cab. I think he hated that I was going to the Statue of Liberty. He probably knew that I'm a tourist. What I didn't know was that you had to take a goddamn boat out to see the statue. It seemed like a waste of time, but I bought a ticket anyway. I imagined this was the only time that I'm going to be in New York City, so riding on a powerboat with a bunch of other goon tourists, will be a one-time thing. I promised myself that after I saw Ol' Lady Liberty, I would get drunk for a week straight. After about a week, I'm ready to leave any place I visit. I'm kind of a restless soul. If you stay too long, you get tired and start missing home. The boat ride wasn't bad. The tour guide told some funny stories, at least. I didn't even need to wear my coat.

I hadn't checked my phone in a while. I know my parents are going crazy. I admit I'm a selfish bastard. When the boat got to the statue I glanced at my phone. I had like a hundred text messages and there were several missed calls from my Dad. What surprised me was that I had a message from Amber. She said that my parents contacted her parents to see if she might know where I am. The good thing is Amber doesn't know I'm in New York. She said my parents are freaking out. I already know that. If anything, she is thinking about me. I had become the center of attention. I feel redeemed in a sick way, but I still turned the GPS off on my phone.

I can't say that I'm impressed with the Statue of Liberty. It looks more like a green giant with a crown on. People think it represents freedom and the American way. It represents war and bombing the crap out of countries. France probably wanted to get rid of it. We took the goddamn boat back and everybody was quiet. Some of the older people on the boat were starting to tear up like they had seen something important. I wasn't sure what I saw except for a waste of money.

The first thing I did after getting off the boat was find a hotel. I'm paying for everything with cash so I must look like a high roller. The Texas Kid. My Dad likes old Steve McQueen movies. Everybody says that he looked like him when he was younger. I didn't know who Steve McQueen was until my Dad showed me a few of his movies. I like Steve McQueen's style. He didn't care what happened. That's why women love him. Women like to chase and have a challenge. It's the opposite of what I'm doing with Amber. Me being an idiot and spilling my guts to her. Telling Amber how I feel is probably one of the dumbest things I've ever done. Steve McQueen would never do that.

Anyways, after checking into my room I decided that I would walk around and find a bar.

I should also mention that my Mom is a big Kris Kristofferson fan. I grew up listening to some of his records and he sings something about being a walking contradiction. I think it means you do the opposite of what you believe in. I'm always doing that. I say one thing when I mean the other. I do that a lot when I'm messing around with people. In New York City, you must be careful about who you mess with. If you piss off the wrong person, you may end up with a bullet in your head, or worse. In Texas, everybody has guns. I mean everybody and their grandmother. That's why Texas is a polite state.

I did another dumb thing and that was going to Times Square. I've seen it on TV many times with that big ball on New Year's Eve. Everybody gets excited because they survived another year. I didn't stay long. The screens flash all day, and people stand there, mesmerized like a bunch of idiots. I needed a drink.

I left Times Square and walked around a little more until I saw this bar. The name of the bar wasn't original. It's called "NYC Bar". It's a craft beer bar. I don't care for the stuff. I like lagers that you can get really drunk on. The bartender seemed like a good guy though, he didn't ask for my ID. I told him to give me one of the beers that were on special. I had three of them and got wasted. It turned out to be one of those strong craft beers with high alcohol content. I paid my tab and left the bartender a good tip. I stumbled out of the bar and found a subway station. I don't remember much except I ended up at Central Park.

The sun was still barely up. I'd read a little bit about Central Park, so I knew it was a beautiful place. This garden that's in the middle of all the filth and scum of the city. It seems like an innocent place but I'm sure they find plenty of dead bodies in it. That's the thing when you find something perfect, there's always something that ruins it. What I did was find this place where I could lay down on the grass and pass out. I looked up at the stars and I thought about Amber. I also thought about what a selfish bastard I am. I needed to go home but something told me not to. I needed a new life.

4

I woke up because somebody was kicking me. Some cop came along and tried to wake me up. I was hungover. I had a smirk on my face and the cop told me to get up. Things could have gone a lot worse. I got up and saw a bench. There were these pigeons and before I knew it, I was surrounded. They expected me to give them something. I was sobering up so after messing with the pigeons, I decided to start walking back to the city. I walked for a couple of miles but then I got a taxi. This driver was friendlier than the one from yesterday. He was chatty and annoying. I asked him why the pigeons and rats were so goddamn big in this city.

"How the hell should I know kid, but you know it might be in the water," he said.

"I heard that about pizza. The water is what makes the dough so great," I said.

"Yep, New York has the best pizza in the world. The rats and pigeons might be fat because of the pizza."

I laughed about that one. I never found out his name. I didn't even look at his name tag by the steering wheel. It felt good to talk to somebody. It's always good to talk with someone when you don't have to ever see them again. Things aren't like that with Amber. I want to see her again. Not only that, I can't get her out of my head. When I can't get things out of my head that's when things go wrong. Love can mess you up.

There was a liquor store close to the hotel. I planned to go back to my room and get drunk. I don't care about anything really. I figured if I could get wasted then I wouldn't have to deal with the pain in my heart. I was staying at the famous Chelsea Hotel. When I checked in, I asked the guy behind the counter if Janis Joplin's room was available. He said no but gave me a room that was close by. Inside, I eyed up the phone book. The only reason I know a phone book exists is that my grandmother has one.

This phone book was different. It had these sex ads in the back. Most of the girls looked trashy but some of them looked hot. I was drunk so I dialed one of the numbers. To my surprise, somebody answered. They said they were sending a girl to my hotel room. I told the guy on the phone my name was Maurice. I thought it sounded suave. My Dad always uses that word. When he likes something, he says that's pretty "suave". I told you my Dad isn't that bad of a guy. I kept drinking but then I heard a knock on my door. I didn't even really know what I had done. I'm pretty sure prostitution is illegal but honestly, I was so drunk I didn't care.

I looked through the little peephole in the door and there was this woman outside. She had on this tight black dress and she looked rather good. I hesitated to open the door but then the alcohol took over.

"Are you Maurice?" she asked.

"Yes, I'm him." I must have sounded dumb because I was slurring my words.

"You look like some kind of a loser," she said.

"I am on earth but not in heaven."

Those words surprised me because it felt like someone was speaking through me. It was strange but then again it might have been the whiskey. I don't think it was a spiritual experience. Nothing spiritual about being in hell. The prostitute laughed in my face and left. It reminded me of my relationship with Amber. Nobody takes me seriously. I decided that from now on people would take me seriously. I'm not sure what I'm going to do, but I'm going to do something important. I want to be infamous.

**

I didn't do much in the next few days except sit in my room and get drunk. I hated the city. There are too many people here and nobody has any sense of humanity. I'm sure there's a few that do, but overall, I haven't seen anything that gives me hope. I can say that about most places. I turned my phone off most of the time. Having nobody to talk to can sometimes be great. I mean eventually, you get tired of it, but it's nice to be alone. The only problem is you start feeling like a creep.

I wanted to do something you see in those old movies. You always see these guys hopping trains and riding out to California. There's a sense of adventure in the whole thing. I started to feel guilty about not telling anybody about leaving. One day, eating a thick pepperoni pan pizza from some hole in the wall shop, folded, I texted my Mom and told her that I was doing fine. I told her that I needed to get away and that I was sorry for disappointing them. I told her I would be home soon and not to worry.

I did want to go home at some point. I decided to rent a car. My fake ID was better than my passport. I had access to anything in this crazy country. Nobody questioned me. I know Kerouac is buried in Massachusetts. His hometown is Lowell which used to be an old mill town but now is infested with drug addicts. This country has become a goddam wasteland. It seems everywhere you go, everybody's hooked on meth or smoking crack. It's disgusting and the government likes it. If they can keep the people dumbed down and bring in all the drugs, then they have control.

It was hell driving out of New York City. I don't know how many toll roads I ran. I can see why people commit suicide. Everything seems so cold and indifferent and there's just scum on the street. The government nickels and dimes you to death.

My favorite character in Kerouac's, *On the Road,* is Dean Moriarty. I'm obsessed with the book. Turns out Dean is based on a real guy named Neal Cassady. Cassady was a real rebel and inspired Kerouac's writing style. Kerouac was a madman but from what I've read he was nothing compared to Cassady. Anyways, I found Kerouac's house, and to be honest it was disappointing. Lowell is depressing and I can see why the place is infested with addicts. The corporations moved in and gutted all the industry. All the mill workers got laid off and started doing drugs and drinking themselves to death. Kerouac eventually drank himself to death, too. Maybe that was going to be my fate.

I was thinking about all these things when I decided to drive up to Maine. I know it's a pretty state. I've seen some pictures of it. The thing about being up here is you can drive through three or four states in an hour or so. You can drive like hell all day in Texas and still be in Texas. I wasn't sure where I wanted to go to Maine. I picked a city named Solon because it shares the same name as my Grandfather, Solon. That's an old school name. I think people had cooler names in the past. That's one of the few good things about history. The rest of it is a bunch of wars and people getting upset over shit that doesn't matter.

**

Solon is a nice little city. They have a grocery store and a post office. I stopped at a gas station and asked what there was to do in Solon. The guy behind the counter laughed at me. He told me that if I drove a few miles out of town there was a nice river. I got back in the rental car and started driving north. I passed a porta-potty business on the way out of town. I had to laugh at that because it's a perfect analogy for society. At the end of the day, it's all about shit. You always must deal with shit. I bet the guy that owns all those shitters is a genius. People always must take shits so he's likely to be in business for a long-ass time.

I couldn't find the river, but I saw a sign about a pond. I took the exit and went a couple of miles and sure enough, there was a pond. It was hot and muggy outside, and the damn mosquitoes nearly ate me alive once I got out of the car. I had to walk through some woods to get to the pond, but once I got there, the mosquitoes weren't bad. There wasn't anybody there so what I did was strip down to my underwear and jump in the water. It felt good and I floated on my back awhile and looked up at the sky. It was the bluest sky I had ever seen. I could almost picture Jesus walking out on one of the clouds. I didn't think about it too long because my mind drifted back to Amber. It seems she's permanently stuck in my brain. I wished I could have stayed in that pond forever. I felt good but knew it wouldn't last.

I got back in the car and started driving back to Solon. I was freezing my ass off because I didn't have a towel and I was still dripping wet. I pulled over at this truck stop in New Hampshire and got a greasy hamburger. I checked my phone. Of course, my parents were thrilled that I sent them a message, but they wanted me home. The next thing I did was to check train schedules.

There was a train station in this little shore town in New Jersey. I planned to ditch the rental car there and then take a train to Denver. I didn't realize that I'd have to switch trains three or four times. My geography isn't that great, and Colorado is a long-ass way from Jersey. I stopped at the store called Wawa and just ditched the car there. I got a pack of cigarettes, a Coke, and snacks for the trip. Some lucky bastard is going to find the rental car wide open with the keys in the ignition. I bought a train ticket on my phone and then walked towards the station.

The first stop was in Indianapolis and we had an hour layover. I smoked a few cigarettes and sat on a bench close to the train station. I slept a little bit on the train, so I was feeling better. I thought about how I didn't have a future. There will probably be another war soon and with my luck, they'll reinstate the draft. I'd sit my ass in the desert and wait until my sergeant told me to kill somebody. The train got moving again and I went back to sleep. I haven't had a dream in forever, but the nightmares are always there. It seems you get those for free. I usually have the same one where I walk into the high school and start shooting everyone. I'm not sure why I keep having this nightmare. Maybe everyone is right about me being a certified head case. I wish I could dream more about Amber. At least in dreams, things aren't real, and you can be happy and everything. In real life, you never get the girl, and even if you do, she still doesn't belong to you.

Next was Kansas City. The place is supposed to have a good barbecue, but I think it sucks. Nothing beats Texas barbecue, which of course is all about beef. In Kansas City, it seems kind of like a mix of everything. And in the South, it's all about pork. I can't eat pigs. They're dirty animals that sit in shit all day. You always see these obese chefs on the Food Network bragging about their regional cuisine. I know this because my mother binge watches all these shows on the weekend.

It's pretty easy to be a good cook nowadays all you need is somebody that can cook for you. It's not like it used to be when a woman could cook and clean. Things changed when they all wanted to change the world back in the sixties. Most of the sheep public don't realize that you can never change the world. It's always going to be for the rich people and if you're not rich then you're shit out of luck.

5

The first thing I did when I got to Denver was smoke a cigarette. I found a nice hotel downtown within walking distance of a lot of bars. I didn't plan on turning my phone on for a while, which is hard for me to do, because usually when I'm home, I check it about every ten seconds. Most of us are always on Snapchat. A couple of years ago some of the girls that graduated sent us nudes. The parents made a big stink but every guy at school was thrilled to death.

The more I had my phone turned off the less I missed it. I mean people made it centuries without having smartphones. Hell, most of the people that lived on earth never even had a telephone. If you ever read some of the letters that the soldiers wrote in the Civil War, you can see how dumb our society is. I forgot to tell you that my Dad is a big Civil War buff and we watched this documentary about it on public television. The vocabulary they used in those letters makes everyone look like a bunch of morons today. One of my favorite letters is from a Union soldier who wrote to his wife and told her he loved her and if he never saw her again, she would always be in his heart. The poor bastard got shot a couple of days later. Something crummy always happens when you tell a girl you love her. It's a big turn-off and like a dumbass, I've already told Amber. I'm probably too young to know what love is but we had to read Romeo and Juliet junior year. I know now Juliet killed herself because Romeo got all mushy.

I didn't feel like renting a car in Denver, so I just walked around to all the bars and got drunk. I took a bus and went to Pike's Peak. It felt good standing on top and looking down at everything. I kind of know how God feels now. He probably looks down at his creation and regrets his failed experiment. No wonder everything is messed up when the scientist has abandoned the lab.

**

My last night in Denver I got drunk and made the mistake of calling Amber. I knew she wouldn't answer and then immediately tell my parents that I called. It was the first time that I thought about calling her a bitch. I hated myself for thinking that but I'm bitter because I know it will never work.

I should probably tell you how it all began. I mean with Amber. I was a sophomore when she was a senior and we had an art class together. I noticed her right away because of that red hair. I told you I have a thing for redheads. There's a fire they have that makes my heart stop. I wasted a whole year because I was too scared to talk to her. I figured with her being older she wouldn't be interested in a loser like me. Riley, Taylor, and I were really into skating back then. We'd skate everywhere but enjoyed skating the places where you weren't supposed to. The cops would come and tell us to go home but the next day we'd be back skating again.

Riley and Taylor like Tony Hawk but my favorite skater of all time is Jim Greco. I like Greco's style and he used to be a real drunk. Even when he was wasted, Greco could still get up the next day and do things most skaters only dreamed about. I'm telling you all this skating shit because that's how Amber noticed me. I was kind of showing off in the parking lot doing some tricks when Amber and a group of her friends walked by. I like showing off because I'm a good skater.

Anyways, I noticed Amber looking at me, and then she smiled. That's when I knew that she's the one. I wouldn't say that I stalked her, but I started purposely showing up at places I knew she would be. I think she knew I liked her. Girls have this sixth sense about them. They get in your head and they know what's going on inside of it. The thing was that Amber had a boyfriend. His name is Jason White and he was the big star quarterback. Riley, Taylor, and I all think he is a giant douchebag. I admit we had some fun egging his car and one time we let the air out of his tires. We laughed our asses off about that one.

Most girls are super emotional, but I noticed Amber was crying a lot. I think she's a bit of a drama queen, but most teenage girls are if they don't get their way. I found out that Jason broke up with Amber. It didn't break my heart because Jason White is a total asshole. Amber deserves better. She deserves someone like me. You probably already know by now I'm a hopeless romantic.

I decided to leave Denver because there was a cold spell coming on. One of those once in a couple of years where the lying weathermen get paid to ruin your day. I needed to get back to Texas and besides, I didn't want to spend all my money. I had been living it up. When you get drunk every night and end up ordering nice meals, things add up. I even thought I sprained my ankle about a month ago and all the walking around has left it sore. I needed a break from myself.

**

I found a flight and flew back to Dallas. I didn't want to go home but at least I was back in Texas. A Texas country singer has a song named "London Sick Blues". The lyrics are genius. The chorus is, "I want to go home with the armadillo. Good country music from Amarillo and Abilene. The friendliest people and the prettiest women you've ever seen". They don't make country music like they used to. Today it's all bubblegum crap with a bunch of guys dressed up and glamorous. Waylon Jennings would kick all their asses if he was still alive.

I stayed at a cheaper hotel this time that's close to Deep Ellum. The area had been fixed up by the city. It used to be a cool place to go with a bunch of bars and great live music. There was something seedy about the place which kind of added to its appeal. Back in the late 1800s, Doc Holliday practiced dentistry in Deep Ellum. It used to be the home of real outlaws but now it has a Chili's and a goddamn Chipotle. They really have ruined everything.

I found a bar called the Gypsy Tea Room. They had some cool bands too, but I don't remember any of them. One night, I got piss drunk and stumbled back to my hotel. I always carry a pocketknife. I've done it before, but I took the knife and cut the inside of my arm. It felt good to feel something. Sometimes it takes bleeding to really feel alive. I've cut and scraped myself many times while skating. It's different when you do it on purpose because there's always a reason. You must have pain in your heart to do something like that. I don't want to dwell on it too much. I got drunk a few more days and saw a few punk shows. Then I decided to do something that I've always wanted to do.

I wanted to hop a boxcar and see where it would take me. I turned on my phone and looked up a few train routes. I would wait until night and then see if I could hop one. I went to a local sporting goods store and got a few supplies. I also loaded up on snacks and some water. I took a taxi to the train tracks. I read that some of the trains went to California.

It was easier than I thought to hop on a train. I felt like I was on an adventure. I told you earlier that I don't read many books but one book that they make us read is *Grapes of Wrath* by Steinbeck. I admit I kind of felt like one of the Okies headed out to California. I figured by now my parents were going ape shit and everybody was looking for me. I like the selfish attention. I knew by now that Amber had probably called my parents and told them I tried to call her. I missed my graduation. I missed Riley and Taylor too, but I figured they would understand what I was doing. They may have been the only ones that did.

I sat inside that boxcar for a long time but then the train started rolling. I knew the train was headed west but I had no idea what its destination was. I felt the train was a new friend. I didn't try to get too emotional about it. I decided to let it take me wherever. I hate to keep bringing up books, but you could say this is kind of like *The Adventures of Huckleberry Finn*. Some school libraries still ban it. I can't think of anything dumber than banning a book.

**

The sun shone through the boxcar's door. I had an awful headache, but I sat up and tried to figure out where I was. As far as I could see there was nothing but desert and a few mountains. I thought I was in New Mexico or Arizona. I felt more alone than I've ever been. The train stopped so I got off to see what was going on. I walked for a little bit and then I saw this sign that said Clayton two miles. I was in New Mexico. I didn't feel like getting back on the train, so I walked towards Clayton. I needed a decent meal and a drink. The first thing I noticed was the place is a shit hole. There is hardly anything there, just an old gas station and a deserted Dairy Queen. I saw a sign that said, Eklund Hotel, since 1875.

I decided to walk over there and see if I could get a room. The place had an old saloon and there was this lady behind the desk. She looked like she was about ninety years old and not happy that I walked through the door. She told me that they had rooms, but it didn't seem like a hotel. There was nobody there, so she took me on a tour. The saloon was cool but there were no seats at the bar. The lady told me that it is a stand-up bar just like they had back in the Old West. Those poor bastards back then didn't even have a place to sit when they wanted to get drunk. I sat down and ordered their Armadillo Eggs. They turned out to be stuffed jalapenos. I ended up asking the one old lady server if there was a bar in town. She said the only place was the VFW about a block away. I went up to my room and took a shower. I felt better and then I walked on down to the only bar in town.

I've never been in a VFW, but it turns out, you must sign in and show your ID. Some old veterans were sitting at the bar. I think most of them fought in Vietnam. I don't know much about it except we lost. I feel like anytime there's a war everybody loses. The barmaid was nice, and I felt at home right away. I like cheap lager beers and one of my favorites is Dos Equis. One thing about the place is they have a kick-ass jukebox. I'm a music freak. One of my favorite groups is The Smiths. I only know them because my art teacher played them in class. I found all their music on Spotify and was immediately attracted to the guitar sound. They seem to have happy music with morbid lyrics. I found a few of their songs on the jukebox and played my favorite. Their song "Heaven Knows I'm Miserable Now" pretty much sums up how I feel most of the time. I lost track of time and I must have had a twelve-pack of beer. The girl tending bar looked good. She told me she turned twenty-one next week. I don't remember much after that, but I left with her.

Nikki was her name. She lived in an RV park that wasn't far away at all. I was drunk out of my mind and my thoughts raced like a machine gun. We started kissing and I took Nikki's top off. I kissed her a few more times and then I sat up on the bed. I started crying and Nikki asked me what was wrong. I couldn't find the words to tell her. I ruined the mood by getting mushy again. Nikki said she would make some coffee. We stayed up all night talking about our lives. I told her about Amber and how she was driving me crazy. Nikki told me that being in love is never a bad thing.

6

When I got back to the hotel room my backpack, which had my clothes, phone, and money, was gone. I should have taken it with me. The same lady was at the desk looking pitiful and done with the world. We had a back and forth and I stormed out to clear my head. I could wait around until a train came and go back to Texas. I had a little cash on me but not much. I bought a couple of water bottles and some granola bars. I wasn't sure what I was going to do next, but I did see a brochure at the hotel that mentioned something about this volcano. It's about fifty miles south of Clayton. I decided that I was too far from the train station to make it. I decided to hitchhike and see if I could get a ride to the volcano. I walked a couple of miles and then a truck pulled over and I got inside. I told the guy that I wanted to go to the volcano, and he said that that wouldn't be a problem because he was going that way. I didn't say much to the guy driving the truck and soon I was at the entrance of the national park. Before I left Clayton, I had gotten a little duffle bag at a store and put my water and snacks in there.

I was going to have to hike a little bit to get to the volcano. Of course, when I finally got there, people were everywhere. There were groups of Boy Scouts and a lot of Asian tourists looking around. I should have known better because people ruin everything. They had several trails, but I decided to take the one that went straight to the top of the volcano. It wasn't a bad hike and I passed a couple of girls that looked pretty good on the way. I would have taken them right there on the trail. I hiked a little bit until I got to the top. I could see for miles. The view was beautiful and for a moment I felt like the king of the world. The king of nothing matters, maybe.

I drank some water and then walked back to the park ranger station. The girl working the desk told me they have buses that stop every hour. She said some went to Dallas and some to Colorado. I pulled a quarter out of my pocket. If it lands on tails, I'll go to Colorado, and on heads, back to Texas. For some reason, I was thinking a lot about that kid James, the one I told you about that might shoot up the school. I wanted to plot out his whole crusade, but for me. I would take a shotgun and 9mm and start blasting away. I know the cafeteria is the best place. In my dream, Amber is sitting with all the cheerleaders eating lunch. She makes eye contact with me and I smile like the devil. Then I open fire and kill her and all her friends. Everything after that is a blur. I think it might be symbolic like I'm trying to kill the love that I can never have. Then again it might be that I'm going crazy. A few years ago, my Mom tried to get me on Prozac, but I refused and ran away. I ended up going over to Taylor's house to get drunk, but my parents didn't press the issue after that. I realize now they were only trying to help and honestly, I might benefit from being on medication to help my mood swings. Sometimes when you're at your lowest you only want to go lower.

I kind of forgot about my parents and everything back in San Antonio. The quarter must've known because it landed on heads, so I got on a bus and went back to Texas. I knew where I wanted to go next. There's a city in the Big Bend area called Marfa. It's totally different from the rest of the state with maybe the exception being Austin. The main thing that makes them similar is that they both have an independent spirit. You can probably say that about Texas in general, but

Marfa has freedom. First, it's out in the middle of nowhere and the landscape resembles something like where "Planet of The Apes" was filmed. It's not a complete desert as there are mountains and it surprisingly gets cold at night. I know about Marfa because my Dad used to take us there when I was a kid. The place reminds me of Sam and that's the main reason I decided to go. I wish sometimes that I could go back in the past. I would make everything right and of course, tell Sam how much I love him. I think most people cling to the past and wish they could change things. People that say they wouldn't change anything are full of shit.

**

When I got off the bus in Dallas I stayed at the station and bought a ticket to Midland Odessa. The armpit of the state but it isn't too far from Marfa. I could rent a car and drive from there. I felt like an outlaw on the run.

The people that ride the bus are all the same. They look tired of life and their faces tell stories nobody wants to hear. I suppose that no one wants to hear mine but I'm telling it anyway. The ride to Midland Odessa is a vast wasteland of brush and desert. It's a part of Texas that nobody wants to visit. Both cities are built on the oil and gas industry and they stay in a perpetual smell of rotten eggs. They are boomtowns because when the price of oil is up, they both consist of trailers everywhere that the "roughnecks" live in. When this happens, the goddamn barber can make a hundred bucks an hour. Some whores follow the roughnecks. I know about all this shit because I read about it in Texas Monthly.

I rented a car in Odessa and headed south. I should probably tell you that Midland and Odessa are different cities but all you need to know are they are both shit holes. Marfa however is its own planet. It's full of trust fund hipsters, artists, freaks, and outcasts on the edge of death and the earth. I've always thought it would be cool to live there but like any other place you eventually get sick of it. Jagged red mountains litter the landscape with a scrub brush as far as you can see. Marfa is mostly known for the locale where they filmed the movie "Giant" starring James Dean. I know about it because like I said my Dad used to take us down here. There's an old hotel on the Marfa town square that's kind of a shrine to the movie. It was the last movie that James Dean was in because he died in a car crash before the film came out. It's true what they say, "Die young and leave a beautiful corpse." That's the goddamn awful truth and anybody that says differently is an old sappy bastard.

I still had some cash, so I stopped at a liquor store before heading into the wasteland that is the road into Marfa. I got two six-packs of Coors and a pint of Cutty Shark. The first thing you see when you pull into Marfa is this old motel. It's a place that's cheap and scummy. I parked the car and looked up at the neon sign that flashed Riata Inn. One time, Riley and I stayed here when we ditched school for a week, and there were bloodstains on the sheets. I imagined someone getting chopped up with an ax in that bed. The motel was damn near empty. I recognized the greasy bastard that checked me in last time. That was a few years ago but everything looked the same. How the motel stays in business baffles my mind, but I bet they're selling drugs or providing whores for the Border Patrol.

There's always something shitty going on behind the facade especially when rich trust fund kids are involved. Unfortunately, Marfa has become the hotbed for these spoiled brat hipsters that sit around and drink Topo Chico all day and bask in their parents' wealth. There is a culture war going on today mainly between the old rich Baby Boomers and the crybaby Millennials. I don't think there are any bigger pussies than the Millennials except maybe my generation. If I could have been born into any generation it would have been Generation X. They have all the kick-ass music like Nirvana and Alice In Chains plus they are known as the punk rock slacker generation which I identify with. Everything today is plastic and has long sold out to the corporations for the goddamn almighty dollar. All the music today is shitty pop crap and even punk bands like Green Day sound like Taylor Swift.

Anyways, I checked into my room and didn't notice any blood on the sheets. Then what I did was get good and drunk. I sat by the pool which resembled a toxic waste dump with armies of fire ants lined up in rows. I stared at them for a long time and then I walked down the hill into Marfa. I had a good buzz and it wasn't too long before I arrived at one of my favorite bars, The Lost Horse Saloon. It's the kind of place the locals' hangout at and the guy that owns it wears an eye patch. He always looks pissed as if you're entering his sacred world of wanting revenge for being born.

"Where are you from?"

The voice startled me and when I turned around this cute brunette was there in cut-off jeans and a white t-shirt that was tied in a knot above her belly button. She looked sexy as hell. It seems every time you're hung up on a girl another one comes your way.

"My name is Kellie."

She extended her hand and like a gentleman, I returned the favor. For a moment, I didn't know what to say but nervously I told her my name. She said that Peyton sounded sophisticated and I laughed at that one. My mind did what I didn't want it to do. It drifted to Amber and the trouble I was in by skipping graduation.

I bought Kellie a few beers and we sat down at a patio table. The stars in Marfa seem to be brighter than when you see them in a big city. San Antonio was voted the fattest city for like three years in a row and I doubt if anyone would even care about gazing up at the stars. You can't breathe in a big city. It's kind of the way I felt when I was up in New York. After a few days, you feel all miserable and want to leave because the mass of humanity drains you. In Marfa, there aren't many people. I mean if Beyoncé is doing a photoshoot there, I bet a bunch of morons will gather, but other than that, it's nice year-round. I should probably tell you that Prada Marfa isn't a real store. It's an art project some nut did that looks like a store. It's got real shoes displayed in the window and the idea behind the thing, is eventually it will decay on itself. People in Marfa are always doing weird things. The last time my Dad took us here, the guy at the food truck gave change in fifty-cent pieces. That got to me and even my father got a kick out of it.

Kellie told me she just finished her freshman year at Texas Tech. She's studying to be a nurse. It seems all women want to do something great but most of them end up marrying some rich asshole and spit out a few kids. I thought about telling Kellie that I was supposed to be going into Texas Tech but figured that keeping my mouth shut was the best thing to do. For once, I was doing what I believed. I wasn't getting all mushy as I did with Amber. I was piss-drunk, but Kellie suggested we walk on over to the Marfa Lights.

That's another thing that's strange about Marfa. The famous mystery lights that appear at random times. It's a big tourist attraction with a viewing area. A long time ago, they thought they were locals sitting in their cars turning their headlights on and off. Some scientists think the lights are natural gasses that emit glowing smoke at night. The conspiracy theorists think they are UFOs trying to communicate with us. If the aliens only knew how shitty humanity is, they would have given up long ago.

I walked with Kellie and put the charm on her. I put my arm around her, and she didn't resist. This was turning out to be a banner night. Luckily, the viewing area was empty, and you could see for miles. Then it happened. Kellie leaned in and kissed me. I no longer cared about seeing some damn lights. I felt brave because the alcohol had taken over and I kissed Kellie. We must have made out for a good five minutes and I even put my hand inside her shirt. Kellie didn't stop me, but the funny thing is you never know with women. Kellie pulled away and pointed in the direction of the viewing area.

"I think I see them. Did you see those lights flash over there?"

"Yeah, I think I saw them," I lied.

"Where are you staying?" Kellie asked. "I'm down the hill at Riata Inn."

"That looks like a nice place. Kind of vintage."

"It's a dump but in my budget," I smiled and then leaned in and kissed her. She pulled away, brushed her hair behind her ears, then we continued. Girls drive you crazy doing things like that. For a moment everything seemed right with the world.

7

Kellie was staying at El Cosmico. It's a hipster place that charges a hundred bucks to stay in a Yurt, which, to me, is a glorified teepee. I wasn't surprised that Kellie invited me to stay the night with her. I pictured us laying in each other's arms but like most things, reality has a way of slapping you in the face. And wouldn't you know it, there were a bunch of girls and guys inside the goddamned teepee.

Kellie introduced me to everyone, and some asshole was playing the guitar. He looked like Evan Dando from the Lemonheads. I suddenly felt deathly sick. My brain started going to the dark places that I didn't want it to go.

"I think I'm going back."

"Are you sure?" Kellie asked.

"Yeah, I'm not feeling too good." I half smiled and then walked out of the teepee. Kellie followed me and asked what was wrong. I stopped then turned around and hugged her. My mind went back to Amber for some reason. I knew love defeated me again.

"Let me get your number." Kellie pulled her phone out but then I remembered I didn't have my phone.

I stood helpless in front of Kellie and at that moment, she looked like an angel. These things always happen to me. When everything is going right, I somehow manage to fuck it up.

"I don't have a pen and paper but if you want to meet us for breakfast about ten tomorrow at the food truck," Kellie said.

"I'll see you then and I enjoyed tonight." I leaned in and kissed her. It would be the last time I would ever see her.

I made it back to the motel. The sun was coming up over the mountains when I collapsed into bed. I started thinking about my obsessions again. I couldn't sleep but I seemed to be drifting in and out of consciousness.

The nightmare remains the same. The assault rifle feels good in my hands as I enter the school cafeteria. Amber is there with her friends when I open fire killing anyone in my sight.

I woke up drenched in sweat. I glanced at the alarm clock. It was almost two in the afternoon. I had missed breakfast but more importantly seeing Kellie. I remembered that I still had a six-pack and a pint of whiskey left. I got them out of the refrigerator and broke the seal on the whiskey. I took a few hits and then started on the beer. The last thing I remember was collapsing back into bed. When I woke up it was dark outside. The moon looked blood red and the desert was still there. I got in the rental car and headed north. I drove like a madman with no sense of direction. I decided to head to Marathon. There is an old hotel there and not much more. It's even more isolated than Marfa and if you want to disappear it's ideal.

I checked into the Gage Hotel. I had enough for a couple of nights. I'm not lying when I say there's nothing in Marathon. It does have a small public library and I decided to walk over there after eating lunch. I told you earlier that I'm not much of a reader, but I needed something to calm my mind. I found a chair by a window. I picked out a book by Knut Hamsun called *Hunger*. The cover got my attention. There is a ghastly figure screaming on it. I started reading and soon realized the story is about a writer. The words were easy to read and to be honest I couldn't put it down. I can relate to the main character. He gives up everything for his art even if it means starving to death. His passion is to live by his own rules. I want to do the same but being young there seems to be no way to avoid the conformist society. You go to college and then choose a career path. You slowly become something you never wanted to be. You're a wage slave. The machine gives you just enough to get by and keep you working. And you're supposed to be grateful for making some rich bastard more money.

I didn't finish the book but had a feeling it didn't end well. The librarian kept giving me the eye now and then. She probably knew life had defeated us both. After that, I didn't do much in Marathon. I stayed drunk for two nights and talked with a few locals about what the hell they did. Most of them were retired and wanted to get away from themselves. Their past seems to haunt them and being out in the desert adds to their misery. The place is full of sad bastards waiting on death. With Sam dying so young, death isn't something, I fear. The unknown is always better than the known. That's how I see it anyways.

**

I left Marathon and decided to head home. I owed it to my parents and the thought of seeing Amber again made me smile. I don't smile all that much. Most people fake their smiles. One thing my Dad always says is, "you can tell how a person is by looking in their eyes". There's some truth in that and I think Amber is sad when I stare into hers. Maybe we are meant to be or maybe it's all in my mind. Whatever it is, I need to know for sure, and avoiding reality never works. I had been numbing myself with alcohol and waiting for something to happen.

I stopped at a gas station and filled up. I figured that would get me back to San Antonio. The trip was uneventful. I passed truck stops and towns that were abandoned long ago. Everything is more depressing on the interstate. A concrete ribbon with trucks about an inch away from bringing death. I kept myself from swerving into them. Something kept me going and I hate to admit it's Amber. Once my parents got over everything, I would get in touch with her. For all, I know maybe she's been talking to my parents and misses me. I know my parents are going to kill me once I get home then it's counseling and getting back on track. That bums me out. The thought of talking to a shrink again makes no sense. I've been on antidepressants for a while. The crazy thing is I've been mixing them with alcohol, and it makes me more depressed. The only thing to do is get back and find Amber.

I never made it to San Antonio. The rental car overheated about ten miles outside of Sweetwater. If Odessa and Midland are the armpits of Texas, then Sweetwater is its asshole. The town is known for its annual "Rattlesnake Roundup". It's an excuse to kill every snake in the area and then throw a party to celebrate murdering reptiles. There are fried rattlesnake filets which they say tastes like chicken and even an exhibit where kids can dip their hands in rattlesnake blood and leave their handprints on a wall. You can't make this shit up. Texas is much more than Austin, Houston, Dallas, and San Antonio. To experience the Lone Star State, you must visit its small towns. I decided to hitchhike to Sweetwater. If I can get to Abilene, then I can take a bus home. A trucker picked me up and we went to a truck stop. I like truck stops because they're good and scummy.

I was hungry so I got the all you can eat chicken fried steak. I sat there a while smoking cigarettes and drinking coffee. I wasn't thinking about much but then I realized that I turned eighteen yesterday. It was getting late, so I decided to get a room at the truck stop. I got a shower, but you had to feed quarters into a box to get hot water. I had reached the end. Death couldn't arrive soon enough. My room was next to an adult movie theatre in the truck stop. I heard sounds of people fucking all night and all I could do was close my eyes until sleep finally came. I dreamed that I was on a deserted island with Amber and we made love on the beach. I woke up early and then started hitchhiking to Abilene.

8

It didn't take long to get to Abilene. Another trucker picked me up and I asked him if he could drop me off at the nearest bus station. Texas is a big ass state and it takes about six hours to get to San Antonio but on a bus, it takes ten hours. I only had about fifty bucks left, and the bus ticket cost forty-five dollars. Barely had any money left to snack. I began to wonder what I was going to tell my parents. I guess it doesn't matter. My obsessive thoughts turned to Amber again as the barren landscape passed outside the bus window. I lucked out and didn't have some crummy bastard sitting next to me. I closed my eyes and eventually went to sleep.

**

When I woke up, we were in the Hill Country town of Kerrville. The bus pulled over at a gas station and everybody got out to take a piss break. I got an RC Cola and a bag of spicy peanuts. I was down to my last fifty cents. I was about a hundred miles from home. I walked behind the gas station and lit up a cigarette. I stared out into the darkness of the night and it was the darkest thing I've ever seen. The void blackness seemed to surround me and at that moment I felt like there was nothing left to live for. You must have something that keeps you going even when you feel there's no way out. I got back on the bus. When I woke up the bus was in downtown San Antonio.

I hitched a ride home and my parents opened the door both ecstatic and pissed off. There wasn't much to say except that I was sorry. My Dad gave the talk about how everyone had been worried sick and how the police put out a search for me. My Mom didn't say anything but seemed to cry and hug me forever. If anything, I felt they were both happy that I didn't die out on the open road. I told them that something didn't feel right and that I just needed to getaway. They told me not to worry because I needed some professional help. My Mom mentioned my medications needed to be changed. That's the problem with the goddamned healthcare system in this country, the doctors throw some pills at you hoping your problems go away. They are making a bunch of money from drug companies and could care less if you live or die. I reluctantly agreed to see another shrink and try some new meds if anything to keep my parents off my back. I told them how my phone got stolen in New Mexico and that was the reason that I'd been out of touch. My Dad said that not having my phone was a good thing for now, but word had gotten around that I was back home. I knew Riley and Taylor would be coming around but to be honest I didn't feel like seeing anyone and having them gush about me being back. My Mom set up a meeting with the goddamn shrink twice a week. I almost felt bad about telling my parents that I had no desire to attend Texas Tech in the fall. To my surprise, they said it would be best for me to be at home for a while. That about settled it for me until something else happened.

One night I was sitting in Sam's room looking at the pool in the backyard and smoking cigarettes. I had the window cracked to let the smoke out and I saw this spider crawling on the outside glass of the window. It hung beautifully in the air like a ballerina as the moon reflected its silver web. I must have stared at it for half an hour trying not to think about much. The shrink put me on Zoloft, and I could tell it was doing something to my brain.

I seemed more spaced out and had lost my appetite plus I had a bad case of the shits. Then I remembered that Amber was home for summer break and my Mom said she saw her at the Country Club. I felt like a man possessed by the pain of love. My parents were asleep, so I walked outside and went to Amber's house. I wanted to see her and hear her voice. All the lights were out but the one in Amber's bedroom. I walked over to her bedroom window and tapped on it. It seemed like I stood there forever but finally, Amber came and opened the window.

"What are you doing here?" Amber asked.

"I wanted to see you, so I came over."

"It's one in the morning besides, I thought you weren't allowed to leave the house."

"I can come and go as I please, it's not like I'm in prison," I said.

"Can I come in? I won't stay long. We can just talk."

Amber must have thought that I looked pathetic, but she opened the window some more and I climbed inside.

"Be quiet, my parents are asleep, and they'll kill me if they find out that you're here. Come sit on the bed."

Amber grabbed my hand and I followed her like a puppy. I told myself not to fuck anything up. I needed to play it cool and not spill my guts. I thought about how Steve McQueen would deal with a woman in her bedroom. He never got sappy and talked about his feelings. The funny thing is we didn't say anything. I think Amber felt sorry for me because she brushed my hair out of my eyes. Then I did something the old Peyton would never do. I pushed her back into the bed and started kissing her. She didn't stop me and then I took her shirt off. She didn't have a bra on, and I kissed her breasts. She reached down and started taking my belt off then everything went wrong. For some reason, I couldn't stop shaking. Amber nudged me off her and then hugged me.

"What's wrong?"

It seemed like a fair question from the girl that I've been obsessed with for the last two years. I didn't know what to say so I started crying. Amber's motherly instinct took over and soon we laid down. She held me close and then it started raining outside. We kissed a few more times and then it was over.

"You better get out of here before my parents find out. I'm glad you're okay. I worry about you."

**

Amber went back to Baylor. Riley and Taylor dropped by now and then. They were both going to take their basic courses at the local junior college. I told them that I wasn't going to Texas Tech and that my parents thought it best if I stayed home until I felt better. The thing is I didn't feel better. My new meds had me feeling light-headed and sick to my stomach. The doctor said it would take a while for my body to adjust to the new medication. My Mom seemed to remind me of this daily usually when I was moping around the house. I needed a good kick in the ass.

Then I remembered my skateboards. I needed to get back into the groove of skating again. I turned into a fat ass with all the drinking and eating like royalty out on the road. At least my ankle was feeling better. Getting back on the skateboard would help with that. Amber probably felt disgusted that night when I laid on top of her.

Riley and Taylor had grown out of their skating phase. Everybody was turning into an adult now and leaving behind the excitement of their youth. Everybody had a plan to enter the world and make money. Most of the kids from high school would soon be making more money for someone else. I didn't see how the rat race would lead to anything but a shitty future. The future seems too far off and the past too far behind.

I slowly started skating again and after a few weeks, I was feeling better physically and mentally. I became completely obsessed again. I woke up and started skating and didn't stop until it was dark outside. Pretty soon I was remembering some of my tricks. I pushed myself and began skating downtown. San Antonio has a lot of traffic and often I weaved my way in and out of cars. I wish sometimes a truck would hit me and it would all be over. The pain would be gone, and everybody could move on without me. Skating brings me freedom. My parents noticed that skating brought joy to my life. If they knew the risks, I had been taking they would confiscate my boards. I even got chased by some bike cops when I was skating on the sidewalk by the Alamo. I knew somewhere Davy Crockett was smiling down on me. I'm keeping that rebel spirit alive.

Then one day, I stopped skating. I had no desire to do anything but occasionally go outside and throw rocks. I felt insane and the new meds were making things worse. I started hearing these voices in my head and they were telling me to do horrible things. It got so bad that I rarely left my bedroom. My parents kept asking me what was wrong, but I didn't have the nerve to tell them. I forced myself to read books that I didn't want to read. Anything that would calm the voices in my head and dull the pain. I hadn't spoken to Amber since that night two months ago. In a way, I didn't care much anymore and the thought of her makes me angry. I felt a rage building up. I told my parents I no longer needed to talk to a shrink.

9

About a month later, I started to feel better. I got off the medication and that seemed to help things. I told my parents that I would like to go to Texas Tech in the spring. To my surprise, they thought it would be a good idea. Riley and Taylor had both gotten girlfriends over the summer and I rarely saw them. I tried not to think about Amber and every day it got a little easier.

The thing about Texas Tech is that it's about as far away from San Antonio in Texas that one can get. This did appeal to me in a lot of ways. I decided to live in the dorm that semester. My parents were paying for everything and in some way, I almost got motivated.

Texas Tech is in Lubbock. Lubbock would be another dried-up cotton town without the university. Instead, it has about three hundred thousand people, and pretty much the entire economy is based around Tech. I visited the campus with my Dad and one thing I noticed was all the girls were hot. Greek life is big on campus and if you don't join a sorority or fraternity, you're an outsider. That type of shit isn't me and all I needed to do was focus on passing my classes. Peyton Pieters the "scholar" had a nice ring to it.

My dorm, Bledsoe Hall, is the oldest on campus and at best it resembles a Cold War-era style bunker. The metal bunks are bolted to the floor in the rooms and the only things in them are two desks and two chairs. Mom and Dad helped me move in and then I hugged them goodbye. It felt good to be free but that didn't last long.

"Where are you from?" said my new roommate, Scott Landers. He waltzed into the room like he owned the place, touching all my shit.

"I'm from San Antonio, and yourself?"

"I'm from Dallas, grew up in the Highland Park area."

Scott smirked like a spoiled rich kid and threw his bag on the bottom bunk. I didn't want to tell him I knew about all the rich crummy bastards in Highland Park. Just when life is going sunshine it throws another asshole in your path. Thankfully, I rarely saw Scott as he made it known that he was joining a fraternity. I heard him brag about being a "legacy". It's when you take up after your father in the same fraternity. Scott is one of those pricks that never shuts his mouth. He brags any chance he gets and soon I found myself avoiding him at all costs. I figured out his schedule after a few weeks.

The only time we interacted was when he stumbled in drunk. It was usually two or three in the morning and sometimes he brought a girl. I pretended to be asleep, but I could hear him having sex. It was disgusting and eventually, it got to me. People fuck without love. I read in a magazine that fucking with love is more intense. I confronted Scott about his late-night escapades, and he told me to stop being an asshole. I told him I was going to kick his ass. That shut him up and he stopped bringing them over.

I found myself at the library more often. I never enjoyed reading in high school, but I was thinking about being an English major. That semester I discovered Franz Kafka. My English professor made us read Kafka's short story, "The Hunger Artist". It's about the poor bastard that starves himself for the entertainment of the public. I related to the main character. He seemed to be miserable and nobody knew why or cared that he starved himself. He was just a freak in a cage. In the end, the circus puts him out with the animals and gets a strong hungry panther to take his place. The hunger artist finally admits at the end that he starved himself because he could never find food he liked.

I sat in the corner of the library by myself when I heard a voice.

"You a Kafka fan?" This cute brunette said as she stood in front of me.

"I'm just kind of getting into him."

"You must have Professor Bingham? My name is Jordan by the way."

She extended her hand and seemed generally interested in talking to me.

"I have Bingham in the morning. I came over here to understand what he's talking about in class," I said.

I noticed how she looked. Her hair was tied in a ponytail and she wore denim cut off shorts. Her legs were as sexy as hell.

"You really should read "The Metamorphosis" next. I think you'll like it. I have Bingham in the afternoon," she said.

There was an awkward silence. I kept telling myself not to fuck it up. It's not every day a beauty like her comes up to you.

"I guess I'll see you around," Jordan said. She started to walk away, and I felt my gut-churning.

"Wait, my name's Peyton." I stood up and towered over her. Women love taller guys and Jordan smiled looking up into my eyes. At least this time, I had a new phone.

"Let me get your number. Maybe you can teach me some Kafka sometime?"

I admit my line sounded suave. I was turning into my Dad saying suave too goddamn much.

"Sure, that would be fun."

I handed my phone to Jordan and she put her number in it. We both smiled and she was gone.

I walked out of the library. It was surprisingly warm for January. I thought about how nice Jordan seemed but sometimes you never know until you spend time with a girl. Once you get to know each other that's when all the faults and scars come out. I thought about these things and decided to go on a long walk over in the Tech Terrace area. It's a pretty nice neighborhood and reminds me a lot of Alamo Heights. I walked to a park and many students were laying around on blankets and a few playing frisbee. Our generation has had it too good for too long. We somehow avoided a world war and the economy has been in the biggest bull market for over a decade. It's only a matter of time before the whole shit house goes up in flames. I must have looked strange walking in the park. My hair covered my eyes and I was dressed in all black. I didn't know how long I'd been wearing my tee shirt.

I started to think about Jordan. What if she was just being nice? She probably doesn't like how I dress. She probably hates punk rock too. My mind began to come up with impossible scenarios. It jumped to unrealistic expectations. I knew nothing about this girl. I became crippled with anxiety. Maybe I shouldn't have gotten off my medication. I began to walk faster and didn't stop until I was back at the dorm. I sat on the steps out front and lit up a cigarette. It brought some relief but then I saw him. Scott Landers was walking toward me with a shit grin on his face.

"You are being a loser again, huh?" Scott laughed but sensed that I wasn't in the mood for his bullshit. Something snapped in me and the beautiful red began to run down Scott's face. Scott fell to the ground and I walked over and kicked him in the head. I heard him groan and I walked away.

I shouldn't have done it but for the first time in a while, I felt alive. I just knew security cameras captured the whole thing. It probably wouldn't be long until the cops got involved. I would be charged and sent to the Lubbock County Jail. My brief stint as a college student was over. I walked off campus and went to this club, The Tunnel. It caters to the goth scene which I briefly got into my sophomore year. I didn't realize that it was already almost eight and that I hadn't eaten all day. Food was the least of my concerns, but I had my cigarettes and had just kicked a prick's ass. I went into the club and it was practically empty. There was nothing to do but get piss-drunk. I thought about what my folks would think if I killed somebody. I would be doing the world a favor. Another goddamn waste of a life gone forever. Good riddance.

I texted Amber. It was something that I probably wouldn't do sober. Then, right after, I texted Jordan to get the bad feelings out of my head.

Peyton Pieters the desperate drunk.

I didn't get a reply from Amber, but Jordan texted back almost immediately. I don't remember what I told her, but I left the club and puked in an alley. I started walking back to campus when this car pulled up next to me. It was Jordan. I must have told her to come to pick me up. Jordan knew I was drunk. When I got in the car I reached over and tried to kiss her. She said something about me being wasted and that she wasn't going to let me spend the night alone.

The next thing I knew we were at her dorm. When we got to her room, we started kissing and ended up on her bed. There were stuffed animals everywhere and several fell off the bed when I collapsed on top of Jordan. I don't remember much after that except when I woke up, she was gone. Did I have my first one-night stand? I sat up on the bed and had the worst headache. Jordan left a note that said she went to class and that she would text me later. I put my clothes on and left. I walked past the Student Union building and picked up a free copy of the university newspaper. I normally would never do this, but something told me there would be something written up about Scott.

I flipped a few pages and there was an article. It said Scott was in the hospital in fair condition. Unfortunately, I didn't kill the bastard. I was officially a fugitive. I could deny it but that wouldn't work. I'd tell the police we got in a fight and I lost my temper. With any luck, I'd probably get community service or probation. The thought of it made me want to die.

I went to the campus police office and turned myself in. The worst of it was rotting in a jail cell until I could finally call my Dad. He bailed me out, but I was given a court date in a month. I was a complete embarrassment to everybody. I was finally getting my life together and messed up all over again. Jordan sure as hell wouldn't want to have anything to do with me and the whole thing with Amber was over before it began.

I'll tell you that I got lucky and only got community service. The judge let me off easy because I had a clean record. I thought about how many times I should have been busted for being a public drunk or vandalism. However, a week later, I got a letter from the dean saying I was expelled. Figured as much, they couldn't handle some nimrod like me with a short fuse punching the lights out of anyone who pissed me off. So, what better way than to just get rid of the disease before it became terminal?

Riley and Taylor knew of course and all the kids in the neighborhood were talking about it. It only added to my rebel image. The community service sucked. I had to report to the bastard police officer every weekend. They made me pick up trash on the side of the road for about six months. The hell ended, but by that time, everyone had moved on. I moped around the house and played video games. I went into Sam's room and smoked cigarettes at night. I rarely talked to my parents and when my Mom tried to cheer me up, I only felt worse. Maybe I'm being too hard on myself. There certainly are worse things than beating the shit out of Scott Landers. I just knew he would go on to have a successful life. Rich bastards always have it easier than everyone else.

I was in bed one night when Jordan texted me. It's true what they say about women. You gotta give them space and not press the issue. I wish I had known this with Amber but sometimes you must fuck everything up before you see the light. Jordan didn't seem upset or anything. She told me her roommate knew Scott because of some fraternity parties. Jordan said that everyone hated him. She mentioned that Scott had raped a few girls, and nobody talked about it. This didn't surprise me. I did everyone a favor by kicking his ass.

I was starting to feel better, but wouldn't you know it Amber texted me. She said she was worried and missed me. This time it was different. The feelings I once had didn't matter all that much. I felt nothing. I'm sure there's a spark inside me that's still mushy over her but it's not much of one. That's what scares me. Sparks can lead to fires that burn out of control.

**

I woke up one day and it hit me. I was wasting my time sitting around the house. I'd been talking with Jordan a lot and wanted to see her. I told my parents that I was moving back to Lubbock. I mentioned it was about a girl and my parents said that they were fine with me moving out. They gave me the talk about how they would always be there but that I would be on my own. I would have to get a job or back in school. I was hoping my probation officer would put in a good word so that I could attend a community college in Lubbock. I still didn't have a car, so I'd have to take a bus. I had about a thousand dollars left but that wouldn't last long. I didn't take much except a bag with clothes and my skateboard. I figured if it didn't work out with Jordan, I could always skate to clear my head.

My Dad drove me to the bus station, and I left San Antonio. It didn't take long for my Mom to text me and she said to let her know when I got to Lubbock. The drive to Lubbock is butt ugly but it's even worse on a bus. The whole damn trip old people were coughing and kids crying. It was depressing as hell. I needed to get a car. I needed a new start.

I knew now how the Samsa family felt after Gregor died. Their lives all got better and even that little bitch Grete became a woman. In the end,

Gregor died in the sadness and filth of his room. I realized when I finished the story that Gregor is Kafka. The whole thing is about Kafka's real life and the desperation he felt in his own family. His dad abused him and didn't encourage his writing. Of course, his mother always sided with her husband. Kafka died relatively unknown. but his friend Max refused to burn his manuscripts. If that would have happened, we'd be even dumber as a society. I thought about these things as the bus rolled to West Texas. I ate a few burritos at Allsup's when the bus stopped in Post. It's another shit town in the middle of nowhere.

Jordan said she couldn't wait to see me. The other thing on my mind was if I'd run into Scott again. Jordan can't keep a secret. Girls never keep their mouths shut. Even if it's some gossip about themselves they blab it out to their girlfriends. If Scott found out I was back in town he'd probably get his fraternity brothers to jump me. I was probably worried about nothing because the whole thing happened a while ago. Nobody remembers what happened five minutes ago, much less beyond that. People only care about what they see on their phones because everything else isn't reality.

I met Jordan at her dorm when I got to Lubbock. Tech looked about what I remembered. The Spanish architecture gives the campus a distinguished look, but at the end of the day, it's still in Lubbock. If you want to experience hell you can't go wrong with this city. There's hardly any character in the place. It's a wasteland of chain restaurants and cookie-cutter houses all built in the sixties and seventies. The Bible Belt runs through the South, but Lubbock makes it look liberal. The county was dry up until a few years ago and you used to have to drive out of town to get a beer. That changed when the older generations started dying off.

Jordan said I could stay with her until I found a place and it was with her that I finally lost my virginity. Jordan and I were having sex all the time and after a while you kind of get in a routine. I may be doing it wrong, but Jordan seemed to be enjoying it. It helped that Jordan's roommate moved out. When Jordan went to class I mainly read in the library. I read Kafka's novels, *The Trial* and *Amerika*, which I both found depressing as hell. *Amerika* has some dark humor in it, and I got a kick out of that. I need something to cheer me up. It was amazing to be with Jordan, but I still felt down about everything else. At least she didn't care I was expelled.

I thought about enrolling in South Plains Junior College. It's a school where everyone goes to take their basics before going to Tech. The students there are losers whose grades aren't good enough to get into a four-year university. It was too late to enroll in summer school, so the best thing was to get a job. I have no skills, so I searched for menial work. The first one was a dishwasher at a Mexican restaurant. I told Jordan and she laughed at me.

"Nothing wrong with manual labor, and besides, have you ever had a job?" I asked.

Jordan didn't say anything and rolled her eyes.

"It's something to make money until I can get back in school."

I thought Jordan would be impressed with my ambition. I was wrong. The true colors come out once you start to know a girl. If you could skip the getting to know each other crap things would be much easier. Jordan started to come across as a spoiled brat. She didn't have to work because her Dad had a lot of money and I noticed she started criticizing me. She didn't like the way I dressed and bitched about how I smelled like cigarette smoke. I began to resent it. I started avoiding her and even started skating again. You weren't allowed to skate on campus but that didn't stop me.

10

"You load the dishes here and hit this button. You need to rinse them off first and when you're not doing that you can buss tables."

My manager, Arturo, didn't say much. The scalding water burnt the crap out of my hands, and I was covered in food stains. Arturo said if I did a good job, he'd train me to be a line cook.

My new job at El Coyote catered to the college kids with cheap drinks and greasy enchilada plates. The food is good. The other highlight was taking my smoke break out by the dumpsters. I didn't think about anything and worked mindlessly until my shift was over. Jordan and I were not talking much, and I often came in late when she was asleep. I would shower and then crawl in bed next to her. She'd turn away from me and I'd stare at the ceiling.

I managed to scrape up about a thousand dollars and I told Jordan that I was moving out. She seemed indifferent about it. Once a girl's interest level drops you can kiss your ass goodbye. I found a small studio apartment close to campus. I didn't have any furniture except a coffee table that I bought at a thrift store. I also picked up a mattress and a small bookshelf. I found myself reading more. Whatever money I had leftover at the end of the month went to buying books.

I found some gems at the used bookstores. After reading Kafka, my interest went to the Russians. I read Dostoevsky's most famous work, *Notes from The Underground.* I can relate to the unnamed main character. He hated everything. I even tried Tolstoy's, *War and Peace.* I made it about halfway then decided it was pointless. After a while, you find yourself going insane reading these intellectuals. I moved on to the Beats. I read more Kerouac and got into Burroughs. They show grit in their writing. Then I discovered Bukowski. I enjoy his short simple prose. His poetry tells a story instead of using flowery language. He cuts through the bullshit. I kept drinking heavily. I didn't have enough money to buy any of the good stuff. I got drunk on cheap beer and Mad Dog 2020. I woke up every morning with a hangover and then went to work.

I was bussing tables when Jordan and a group of her sorority sisters came into the restaurant. They sat down at a table close to me and then I heard them laughing. I knew they were laughing at me. I didn't give a shit. Nothing but a bunch of crumbs born with silver spoons in their mouths. I decided to walk over to their table. I told Jordan hello and then walked away. She was cordial but as I walked back to the kitchen they started laughing again. I didn't want it to bother me, but it did. I had ignored Jordan since moving into my apartment. For once, I was standing up for myself. I talked to my parents once a week. I told them that I was just working and trying to save money. They asked about Jordan, but I told them that we were done. I wanted to believe it myself and in some ways I did. My Dad offered to give me some money, but I refused. He respected me for that, and I felt good for about five minutes.

**

The routine of going to work, reading, and getting drunk started to get to me. I liked the idea of being an English major and trying to be a writer.

It wouldn't be long until that dream didn't work out. I was almost asleep one night when my phone vibrated. It was a text from Jordan. The more you ignore them the closer they get. She said she missed me and that it was good to see me at the restaurant. The old me would have replied right away and have gotten all mushy. I ignored her and deleted the text. Not only did I do that, but I deleted her number.

Peyton Pieters the heartbreaker.

After that, I got up and went to the bathroom. I took a good piss and stared into the mirror. I was turning into a real bastard. The weeks and months disappeared into nothing but work and drinking. I applied to South Plains but never heard anything back. When I checked my application's status online it said that it was under review. I even called the admission office and they said they would email me about my application. I knew what that meant. They had an issue with me and most likely it had to do with the whole Scott ordeal. No doubt they knew about it.

When I finally got the email, it didn't surprise me. My application had been rejected and of course, they didn't tell me why. They said that I was welcome to apply next semester. It was all over. This sent me into a dark spiral. So, I stopped going to work. I would never have enough money to live on and what little I had went to rent and booze. I had enough dough to make it for about two months. I decided to call my Grandmother. I didn't know why I hadn't thought of it before. I told her everything was great and that I was looking forward to starting classes in the fall. She said she would mail me a check. I almost felt guilty and no doubt she would tell my parents. They would call me and then I would have to tell them about not being able to get back in school.

My apartment has a little balcony and I began to spend most of my time out their smoking cigarettes and drinking. My parents called of course, and my Dad caved and sent me a check for a thousand bucks. I couldn't bring myself to tell them my application was rejected. Now that I had a little money, I could bide my time for a while until something happened. The adage, *you must make things happen for yourself,* is bullshit. Sometimes you must let the unknown come to you.

When I woke up, I had no idea where I was. My drinking had gotten out of control and I was blacking out every night. Then I realized that I was in Jordan's dorm room. I checked my phone and saw that I texted her last night and invited myself over to her place. It started to come back to me. Jordan picked me up and took me to her dorm. We talked a bit then ended up in bed. I was drunk out of my mind. Things got out of control and the realization that I may have forced myself on her seemed to be hazy. I didn't know what to think or do. When I got out of bed and put my clothes on, I noticed a note that Jordan left on the nightstand. It simply said, "You know what you did".

I couldn't think straight so I walked outside and lit a cigarette. Was Jordan accusing me of rape? I would never do that sober but when drunk I'm capable of anything. I suddenly felt a terror in my soul. I didn't know what to do so I went to a bar and got drunk. Later, I stumbled back to my apartment and collapsed in bed. I was awakened by my phone vibrating. My nightmare came true. It was a text message from Jordan. She said I raped her and that she was filing a police report. I couldn't remember what happened. I genuinely wanted to die. You go all this way to hopefully die a hero, but then you become a villain, or whatever that actor said. Either way, that was me.

II

The police officer knocked on my door a few days later. He told me that Jordan filed a report. I told him that I wasn't saying anything until I talked to a lawyer. It's going to be her word against mine. I called my Dad and he said he would get me a lawyer. I decided to pack my things and get out of Lubbock. I paid for my last month's rent and left the mattress and coffee table in the apartment. The bus ride back to San Antonio was depressing. I didn't like being back home. My parents viewed me as a criminal. I was honest and said that I didn't think I was capable of raping her.

I spent most of my time smoking cigarettes and skating. But I let off drinking so I wouldn't make a big mistake again. My only solace was skating and going into Sam's room at night. It's the only place I can clear my head. Word got around that I was a rapist. Taylor and Riley didn't even text me anymore. I felt like a complete loser.

One morning my Dad woke me up and said a police officer was on the phone. I got some good news, the officer told me Jordan dropped the police report. I knew she was lying the whole time. I felt as if the weight of the world had been lifted off my shoulders. I could see the relief on my parents' faces but we didn't talk much. Something changed when I left to be on my own. I mainly stayed in bed and read books. The thing that messed me up, even more, was that Amber texted me. She told me that she had heard about everything and was glad that it all worked out. I didn't reply.

It felt good ignoring her. I wasn't sure if I had feelings for her anymore or if I was just lying to myself. I knew one thing and that was that I couldn't stay at home. I was depressed and my folks kept asking if I got accepted at South Plains. I told them my application was under review and that I would probably know something soon. I didn't have a problem lying to them. I told my parents I was going back to Lubbock, but instead, went to Fort Davis.

It's in West Texas not too far from the Big Bend. That's the part of Texas that dips down and has many unique towns like Terlingua. Terlingua is where they have the infamous "chili cook-off" that was started by outlaws like Willie Nelson and Jerry Jeff Walker. The place is a ghost town and on the border of Mexico. I wondered someday if I would remember this as my "Kerouac" period. Formal education isn't going to be my path in life. As Neil Young said, "it's better to burn out than fade away."

**

I was running low on money so I did something I never should have done. I was getting bad headaches and couldn't think straight. I bought a bus ticket to Waco. I knew Amber would be back in school. After my newfound confidence with girls, I was going back to my obsession again. On top of that my nightmare was bothering me more than ever. The one where I walk into our high school and start shooting everyone including Amber. In my dream, everything seems different yet so familiar. The school looks different, but I know all the students I kill. There are screaming and blood everywhere. I wake up in cold sweats. Nightmares are just dreams that don't work out.

I didn't even bother telling my parents about anything. For all I knew, they thought I was back in Lubbock working as a dishwasher. The thing about shit jobs is everyone thinks they're shit jobs until something happens that affects them personally. The only time people feel they've been wronged is when it happens to them. Think about all the truckers that haul the food we eat or the nurses that take care of the sick. When those jobs no longer exist, we'll all be wandering around like zombies. People are all selfish bastards and I'm the biggest one. I never felt more like killing myself. How would I do it? A gunshot to my head would be the quickest way to get it over. Then there is hanging myself which didn't appeal to me. The easiest way is to take a bunch of sleeping pills and drink a bottle of red wine. Then again maybe things would get better. My generation doesn't think all that much about the future.

There was this girl Anna in one of my English classes in high school. She was quiet but pretty. I even spoke to her sometimes but one day she was gone. Her parents reported her missing, but a few kids found her hanging from a swing set in a park. The whole school was shocked for a couple of days but then life went on like nothing ever happened. It was like Anna never existed at all. Often people think killing yourself is a selfish act. Nobody considers that maybe the person wanted to die. I don't blame Anna but a society of narcissists that can't take one goddamn minute to listen to anyone or even care about getting to know someone that might be different from themselves. We're screwed as a human race and one day it's all going to come crashing down.

When I got to Waco it was pissing rain. The first thing I did was light up a cigarette and find a bar to get drunk. I knew this Irish pub close to Baylor from my previous visit, so I started with Guinness and then whiskey. I don't remember much after that, but I woke up in Amber's dorm room. She must have come and picked me up after several drunk texts I sent her. I kind of lucked out that she was on campus. When I woke up, I noticed she had sent me a text that asked how I was doing. I felt like I was repeating myself. I was going nowhere all over again.

It didn't take long until Amber told me she had a boyfriend. Why had she been texting me now and then? It soon became clear that she wanted to be a good friend. She told me all of this when she came back from class and honestly, I resented it. Then I did something I shouldn't have. I called her a fucking bitch and she started crying. I apologized but it was over. I left her in her dorm room. Why the hell did I even come back to Waco? Maybe I was trying to fill the hole in my heart or maybe I still had feelings for her? None of it mattered anymore.

What I did after that was take a bus to New Orleans. I had about four hundred bucks left so I got a cheap hotel not too far from Bourbon Street. If ever there's a dirty city, it's New Orleans. From its voodoo bullshit to the puke lined streets during Mardi Gras, it's the ideal place to drink yourself to death. The other place is Las Vegas. I saw a movie once in which Nicholas Cage drinks himself to death in Vegas after losing his job. There's no glamor in the flashing lights or making a sucker's bet with your last dime.

I found a bar named Mickey White's on Rue Bourbon. It seemed to be a local dive bar which I liked right away. The weird thing about it is you must take this ladder to go take a piss. I got drunk out of my mind and on my way to piss, I fell off the ladder and busted my ass. The bar erupted in laughter and I noticed blood coming from my head. I landed hard on the concrete floor. The next thing I knew two cops were throwing me in the back of their squad car. The handcuffs were cutting off my circulation and one of the cops said I was going to the drunk tank. This is pretty routine in New

Orleans and when I got to the jail some nurses came and cleaned up my head. She put spray on my cuts, and it burned like hell. A cop came and took me to a jail cell with the other drunks. I must have looked like fresh meat, so I moved to a corner and curled myself up into a ball. I was still drunk but eventually, I went to sleep. When I woke up there was only one other old guy in there with me.

This cop eventually came and got me. I wasn't charged with anything except public intoxication. I had to pay a fine. It could have been much worse. Instead of playing it safe when I got out, I went back to Bourbon Street and got drunk again. There was no way I could tell my parents about being in jail. Their son had officially become an alcoholic. I couldn't stay in New Orleans but my last night there, I took my pocketknife and cut my arm. It felt good to feel something again. I woke up the next day and went back to San Antonio.

My parents were glad to see me probably because they knew I still needed help. They didn't even ask me about how I hurt my head and arm. I told them things didn't work out and how my application was rejected from South Plains. I'm grateful for my parents. They have a lot more patience with me than I do.

I was disappointed in my so-called best friends. I hadn't heard from Riley or Taylor in a long time. That's the thing about high school, once it's over nobody cares. All the teachers and faculty move on to the next group of students they can indoctrinate. The machine spits you out and then prepares the next generation for their future of misery.

What is there to look forward to in life anyways? I never asked to be born that much I know. I found myself spending more time in Sam's room questioning why he died. It doesn't make sense, but my Mom always says, "God has a plan for everyone." That's nothing but bullshit. What kind of God kills innocent people? What kind of God makes kids suffer in places like Syria? What kind of God turns his back on his people? The whole thing is a lie. The story of Adam and Eve never happened just like the phony part about Noah building a goddamned ark. How the hell did he get all the animals on there? What about the dinosaurs?

**

Fort Davis was on my mind, so it was only natural I went there again. It is named after a real fort. Originally, the Confederates occupied it during the Civil War, and it's named after the president of the South, Jefferson Davis. The Union took over after the war and it was mainly used as a trading outpost and stronghold to fight the Apaches. I kind of know about this because the first thing I did was go to the fort. It's a state park and you can walk around and read all the plaques about its past. I got bored so I figured that I had better find a place to stay. If I had an RV, I would set it up in the park right outside of town, but I opted to stay at this old hotel. It sat right above this old-timey soda fountain ice cream shop and restaurant. I was the only bastard staying in the place.

I checked into my room and then went down to the restaurant. I noticed this beautiful girl waiting on tables. She had raven hair and a slender body. She was looking at me. I smiled at her then walked outside and sat on a bench. I lit up a cigarette and stared at the mountains in the distance. The sunset was a red mad beautiful fire that hung in the desert sky. I smoked a few more cigarettes and decided to head back to my room. I was feeling tired from driving all day. I walked back into the restaurant and she was cleaning the tables. She looked up and brushed her hair back behind her ears.

"Hi." I figured that was the best thing to say.

She didn't say anything for a while but then extended her hand.

"I'm Lauren."

"I'm Peyton, nice to meet you."

We stood there a while and then I told her that maybe I'd see her later. She said she would be working tomorrow night. I smiled and then walked upstairs to my room.

It took me a while to fall asleep. I kept thinking about Lauren. The newness of meeting another one. I'm a fool. If anything, girls added more misery to my life. There had been my complete obsession with Amber the last two years and then the nightmare with Jordan. I had just met Lauren and already I couldn't wait to get to know her. I imagined her a good, hard-working girl, but often, the devil has the prettiest smile.

I picked up a twelve-pack of beer and put them in the fridge in my hotel room. It wasn't long before I collapsed into bed and dreamed about Lauren lying naked next to me. I was awakened by the cleaning lady knocking on the door. I got up and put on my clothes which consisted of my usual black tee shirt and jeans. I grabbed my skateboard and headed down to the restaurant. There was no sign of Lauren, so I went outside and sat down on a bench. I smoked a cigarette and noticed that there wasn't much going on in Fort Davis. I couldn't have asked for a more beautiful day. I sat there a while then I started skating. I didn't think about anything but going as fast as I could. I jumped curbs and went straight down the middle of the street. I took the circular drive that went around the courthouse and I tried to jump on top of a bench. I hadn't tried a trick like that since high school, but I landed it. I started laughing and then I found a tree to lay down under. I must have fallen asleep because when I woke up it was getting dark. At least in Texas, you can mind your business without some shitty cop ruining it.

I went back to the hotel and saw Lauren in the restaurant. She smiled and then I sat down in a corner booth. There was hardly anyone there so Lauren came over and asked if I wanted anything to drink. I told her that I'd take a Coke and some water. She brought the drinks over and to my surprise, she sat down across from me.

She asked how I was doing and why I was in Fort Davis. I told her that I needed to get away from things and my Dad used to bring me here.

Lauren told me she graduated from high school two years ago and was taking classes at the local community college. She said she wanted to go to Sul Ross and study nursing. I lied, saying I was at Tech but decided to just work and save up some money. I didn't want to depress her with all the details. Lauren's black hair kept falling in her face and it was sexy. Her body has curves in all the right places. I suggested that when she got off work, she could show me around town. I knew she was into me, so we agreed to meet in the restaurant in half an hour. I went up to my room and took a shower. I was almost in love again.

There isn't much to Fort Davis, so Lauren and I walked to places that I had skated earlier in the day. We sat down in a park and just enjoyed the moment. Lauren was tough to read like most girls, but I kept her laughing and I knew that was a good thing. She didn't say much but she did lean into me and put her head on my shoulder. It was getting kind of late, so we walked back to the hotel.

I didn't invite her up to my room, yet she followed me. When we got to the room, I got a beer. I gave her one and we sat on the bed. It didn't take long until we started making out. I pushed her back into the bed and then took her shirt off. She reached down and started to undo my belt and then

I got on top of her. I was going to make it, but she sat up and started telling me about herself. I didn't mess up anything because I knew she liked me. We had a few more beers and she ended up spending the night. We didn't do much and eventually fell asleep in each other's arms.

She was gone when I woke up. I didn't even get her number. I knew that I'd see her again, but I was wrong. When I was leaving Fort Davis, I asked an employee at the hotel if she knew anything about Lauren. She said Lauren decided to move to Midland to take care of her grandmother. I thought about trying to get in touch with her, but I decided it was pointless. Of all the places she could have gone, she went to Midland. I hate that fucking place.

12

Austin College is a good school. I'll tell you that my Dad had to pull some strings to get them to approve my application. How it happened was my father knows one of their rich alumni. The guy's name is Mark Lofton. Lofton comes from a family of rich oil bastards. His great grandfather used to work with John D. Rockefeller. I didn't care about that but I'm grateful my Dad made a few calls to help me. Lofton made a big donation to the English Department. If you have enough money you can always help those you want to help. You can also get out of helping those you don't want to help.

When I drove up to Austin, I kept reminding myself of how much I hated it. Too much traffic and goddamn hipsters. Nothing but a bunch of spoiled trust fund kids living out their fantasies on their parents' dime. Most of them go to the University of Texas so Austin College is often considered its little brother. Austin College is primarily known for its academics, but their football team's mascot is the "Kangaroos". There isn't a goddamn kangaroo anywhere except in the zoos. I think it's funny but then again, I could care less about sports.

My parents helped me find an apartment close to campus. The best thing was that I didn't have a roommate. I didn't have to worry about some bastard playing his music too loud or borrowing my food. It was nice being able to walk to campus and I tried to get all my classes in the afternoon. They make you take all the basic classes first, then once you decide what you want to major in, you can enjoy learning. One thing my Dad always says is, "sometimes you have to jump through somebody else's hoops". I didn't realize what he meant as a kid, but now I know it means life is often about kissing somebody's ass to get what you want. Then, later, some bastard kisses your ass and the cycle keeps repeating itself until you die.

I knew right away my favorite class was going to be American Literature. Professor Jenkins has a sardonic sense of humor and that's something I can relate to. Looking back now, it should have been the only class that I took. It sounds cliché, but the first writer we studied was Edgar Allan Poe. They made us read some of his works in high school like "The Raven" and "The Tell-Tale Heart".

Thankfully, Jenkins stayed away from those and we read "The Cask of Amontillado". It's basically about this clever bastard, Montresor, that gets his revenge on a guy, Fortunato. Montresor knows Fortunato loves wine, so he lures him down to his cellar to check out a cask of wine. Once Montresor gets Fortunato down there, he starts burying him alive. Jenkins did a great job of getting into all the symbols and doing what he calls a literary analysis. It's where you have to look beyond the surface of the text to see what Poe is trying to tell us. The best part of the story to me is the irony in Fortunato's name. His name means "fortunate" but getting your ass buried alive is quite unfortunate. I already told you Jenkins' class was my favorite. The thing that I liked about it was it didn't have many students and half the time Jenkins and I were the only ones talking. The other students mainly stared at their phones or played mindless games on their laptops. They were all jumping through somebody else's hoops.

**

Jenkins and I struck up a friendship mainly by having discussions in class. There were a few pretty girls I noticed around campus, but I decided that the best thing to do was focus on my studies. Jenkins got me on to all kinds of books and writers. I got into Jack London and his famous story, "To Build A Fire". Nothing better than reading about some moron that freezes to death because of his foolishness. At the end of the story, the guy tries to kill his dog because he wants to stick his frozen hands inside of it. Talk about a fucked-up way of trying to survive but I suppose when people are about to die, they get beyond desperate. Anyways, the guy finally embraces his death and has a sense of peace about it. The dog gets away and runs on to the other providers of food and fire.

"Hey, Peyton thanks for always being engaged," Jenkins said after class.

"Thanks, I enjoy learning about new writers and then reading them for myself. I'm starting to get what you mean with the analyses and whatnot."

"Listen, a group of students comes over to my place on Friday nights, and we sit around and talk about books. You're welcome to join us this Friday," Jenkins said.

"That sounds like a good time, thanks for the invite."

You bet your ass I was in.

**

Jenkins' place is close to campus and his apartment is swanky. The first thing I noticed was the number of bookshelves. Jenkins has a library in his place. A few other students were sitting on a couch drinking beer and smoking weed. I didn't say much but then finally decided to introduce myself to a cute brunette.

"I'm Peyton."

"I'm Jane, nice to meet you." I held on to her hand longer than I probably should have but she didn't seem to mind.

I soon realized nobody there looked like me. They were all dressed preppy and had a sense of arrogance on their faces. I wanted to relate to them, but something didn't seem right. Jenkins was in the kitchen making a drink but came out smoking a joint. He grabbed a guitar off a table and then sat down and started strumming some sappy folk song. He stopped playing and then introduced me to the rest of the students. The guys had stupid names. One lanky creep named Langston and another frail nerdy guy named Winston. There was another mousy girl named Ashleigh that seemed disinterested in everything. They all kind of nodded and then went back to listening to Jenkins play his song. I guessed this was normal.

This went on a while until Jenkins stopped playing and went back into the kitchen. He brought out some fancy hors d'oeuvres that looked like crackers covered in a brown paste. Jenkins explained them as goose pâté, fattened goose liver and I've read that they stick this tube down the goose's throat and force-feed it grain to fatten it up. It tasted like shit to me, but the bright side was the beer. I'm talking about the good stuff too, not just your plain piss water or the snobby wine-tasting shit. It was right. I didn't care much about that and before you knew it, I was drunk. I don't remember much except that I started to become the life of the party. I got loud and started talking shit with Jenkins. I even smoked some weed and started putting my hands all over Jane. At first, she kind of pushed me away but then she just let me do what I wanted.

I didn't see much of Jane after that and I stopped going to most of my classes. I still went to Jenkins' class but didn't attend any more of his parties. I felt like an embarrassment again, especially in front of those hoity-toity folk. I didn't do much besides drink and smoke cigarettes and occasionally skate on campus. It was sad that no one else did. I guess they were the real academics.

**

It was almost the end of the semester and I had gotten an email from the college saying that I was in danger of failing out. I made a good grade in Jenkins' class but that was it. After reading that letter, I knew I wasn't going to make it, and to make things worse, I was running low on funds. I didn't feel like asking my parents or Grandmother for money again. I didn't want a future or at least one that somebody else had planned out for me. I resisted contacting Amber but one night I got drunk and sent her a bunch of texts confessing my love for her. I knew it was a big turn off, but I didn't care anymore. She tried to pep talk me into trying to pass with C's so that I could stay a student, but I didn't listen. I got a single B and the rest were F's. Austin College and I were no more.

13

"How old are you now Peyton?"

I knew Sanderson was torturing me with this question. He knew my goddamn age but wanted to remind me that I'm an adult. It was his way of showing his superiority and control. People that are in so-called positions of authority are always flaunting their pious superiority in your face.

Once I came back from Austin College, my parents immediately called Sanderson. I flunked out after numerous chances of improvement. My Dad had even called his friend to put in a good word for me. I had disappointed everyone but none more than myself.

"Do you remember the story of Cain and Abel in the Bible?"

This was an unusual question from Sanderson as he usually only asked about my family.

"Of course, I've heard of it." I leaned back in the leather chair and lit up a cigarette.

"Does this bother you?"

I half-smiled like the devil trying to get a reaction out of the shrink. I didn't give a rat's ass if Sanderson hated secondhand smoke.

"So, what do you think of the story?" Sanderson asked.

"It's all bullshit. The Bible is a fairytale based on earlier religions and myths."

If Sanderson wanted to ask dumb questions, then I would oblige him. "What does this have to do with trying to fix my brain?"

Sanderson sat there rubbing his beard and after thinking a few minutes.

"I'm simply curious as to what you think about it. You might find it therapeutic to share your thoughts on it. Your brain is fine, Peyton."

"I'll tell you what I think about the goddamn story. First, people made it up because there was probably this outcast guy in their village. They needed this scapegoat to put all their frustrations on. They made up the name Cain to represent some guy that bullied the hell out of them. This "Cain" was strong and all the other bastards in the village were weak. So, the pussies created this story where Cain took the fall, and Abel represented the weaklings. Of course, Abel would get God's favoritism in the story because the people saw themselves as heroes. Over the years, the story got passed on from generation to generation, so everybody could be a big ass winner and the losers end up in prison or dead. The part about Cain getting some special mark from God leads everyone to believe that he was cursed as well as all descendants. I disagree, however, for Cain's mark was a blessing and made him distinguished. People feared him and he was special in God's eyes. Every bastard that goes to church interprets the Bible the wrong way. They all take it literally when they should look beyond the surface of the text."

"That's very interesting Peyton, do you think about spiritual things a lot?"

For once, it seemed that Sanderson was listening to me.

"I grew up in the church and like I mentioned, my folks are goddamn religious. You'll have to excuse my language, talking about this shit kind of gets me riled up."

"Very well Peyton, is there anything else you want to talk about? Do you have a girlfriend?"

"What the hell does that have to do with anything?" This question burned me up because my mind started thinking about Amber.

"Sometimes, it can help to talk about relationships, but if you're not comfortable, we don't have to go there."

"I don't mind going there. You see, I've been with several girls lately but they're all pretty much shallow. There's one girl that I have feelings about. Her name is Amber, and for the last few years, I've been obsessed with her. I told you about skipping graduation. I skipped going to see her. What I didn't tell you is how I got all sappy around her. That's where I go wrong with girls. I get all emotional and spill my guts too fast. I guess I'm pretty much an emotional guy."

"Sometimes like they say, it's best to play hard to get. Don't feel bad about expressing your feelings. You're not the first man to tell a woman you're in love." Sanderson sat up in his chair and grabbed a pipe from a tin case. "You don't mind if I smoke, too?"

"Hell no, my Grandfather used to smoke a pipe. He's the one that beat the shit out of my Dad when he was a kid. I think pipe smoke smells good. If you're going to light up, then I will too."

Sanderson packed his pipe with tobacco and now we were filling the room with haze. I was beginning to view Sanderson as a father-like figure. You couldn't help but like the bastard. The only difference being, my Dad is paying him a shit load of money to get my head straight.

Sanderson took a puff from his pipe and smiled at me.

"So, Peyton, tell me more about this Amber."

"She's almost two years older than me. I noticed her in my sophomore year. She was the head cheerleader. She was the only reason that I went to the goddamn pep rallies. She didn't know I existed back then, but we ended up talking. In high school, I was a dork, and Amber ran with the popular kids."

"Maybe that's why she ended up liking you, the fact that you two are different. Opposites attract you know."

Sanderson did have a good point.

"Maybe or just the fact that I'm tall. I don't think girls like short guys. They all kind of like to be dominated."

"I won't go there Peyton," he said, holding the pipe far from his head. "But getting back to Amber, are you still, as you say, obsessed with her?"

"I still am because I still think about her all the time. Even when I was with the other girls, Amber is in my head."

"And what is she doing now? Do you still keep in touch?"

"She's up at Baylor in Waco. I went to see her there a few times, but it didn't work. She had a boyfriend at that time, and I'm a jealous guy. Then when I ran off, she kept in touch with my parents. I think she does care about me. I broke down when I was drunk and texted her. We nearly had sex, too, but I ended up balling up and being a wimp. I told her how I feel about her all over again. I have a feeling it's a big turn off."

"There's nothing wrong with expressing your feelings. Peyton. You're young and still not fully developed. You've got your whole life in front of you. If it's meant to be, love finds away. In the meantime, it might help you to branch out a little bit. Being around new people and experiences is what a young man needs. You keep saying you like skateboarding, so why not find some others that do? Throwing rocks sounds a lot like baseball or maybe football, abstractly. Sorry, I'm rambling some, but I think it will help. You've got nothing to lose."

"I appreciate that, but I've never been comfortable around people. I've talked to other shrinks before, and one said I'm socially awkward and probably disposed to alcoholism. I didn't hear back from Amber after my drunk texts. I have to accept the fact that it's over."

"There's nothing wrong with closure and as I said, if it's meant to be it will work out. I think the best thing will be to let her go. If she contacts you great, but you should live your life."

"That's good advice but I'm back home now. I got expelled from one college, failed out of another. There probably isn't a school in the country that will accept me. I had my chance and worse than that, I let my family down. After shelling out all that money, I'm not sure what I want to do now. Maybe I don't want to do anything."

"I understand Peyton but don't get so down on yourself. You're young and making mistakes is part of life. We can learn from them and that's always a good thing. Is the medication helping you?"

You must admire Sanderson, he does seem genuine, but then again, it's not like he isn't getting paid.

"I think the meds are helping. I'm not having my thoughts as much. I wouldn't say they're completely gone but they don't bother me as much."

"That's good and stay away from alcohol. That will make you feel better too."

"I'll try."

"And maybe it's time to do something about Sam's room. If your parents are ok with it, and if you still are there, try making it a shared space. Have parts of you and him in there. That way you can be your true self, without all the grief."

**

I saw Sanderson two times after that, and he told my folks to be in touch if I needed to talk. I think my Dad was tired of paying his ass. I was communicating better with my parents, though. We sat down one night, and I apologized about the expulsion and failing out after they had gone through all that trouble. They said that wasn't important and that they only wanted me to be happy and feel better. It's kind of like a wholesome TV sitcom, where the audience already knows everything is going to work out in the end.

Real-life doesn't work that way and if there's anything I've learned in my nineteen years it's that. I have no idea what's going to happen next. I like that feeling. It's more exciting that way. You can't always play it safe. Sometimes you must charge full steam into shit and then deal with the consequences.

Word must have traveled fast because it seemed everybody and their grandmother knew I'd gone to a shrink for counseling. I should have known Taylor and Riley couldn't keep their traps shut. I'm not even sure we're friends anymore. All we do is get drunk together and play video games. Then they talk about some stupid girls they hooked up with and how they are barely making by in class.

When was the last time they asked how I'm doing? Of course, there is nobody to blame but myself. I shouldn't be so selfish. The end always comes way too early. I didn't do much after that besides moping around the house. I didn't feel like skating or even going into Sam's room. Maybe it's my way of burying the past and hoping somehow my future matters. I do enjoy going on walks in the park. There's this duck pond and I like to sit and watch them swim around. It seems they're going somewhere and nowhere at all.

One day I came home, and my Dad was sitting on the couch with his hands covering his face. I looked at the TV. It was on the finance channel and at the bottom of the screen it said, "Market Plunge". I knew what that meant. My Dad lost a bunch of money but even worse his clients had lost their ass too. It's a lot of pressure when you're in charge of other people's money. They expect you to make them more money and to preserve their initial investment. My Dad says you always need to stay in the market long term. He didn't seem too hopeful when I looked at him. I wasn't sure what to say so I walked past him and went to my room.

I found out later the market tanked because the military assassinated a few generals in Iran. Everybody started talking about war and bombing the crap out of brown people all over again. They say when all else fails, they take you to war. I will never understand why people would want to join the military. I suppose if you're dumb enough to sign up, then that should be the only requirement. I honestly don't care what happens anymore. Sadly, people get so wrapped up in money, they forget to hug the ones they love. Maybe they just don't know what love is. Does anyone?

I got another chance to go to school. San Antonio College will accept anyone if you have your high school diploma, regardless of collegiate issues, which felt like a place for misfits. I could start in the fall semester and I knew now that I wanted to study English. Hell, I'd already been at the public library reading every day anyways. There wasn't anything else to do, so I discovered another writer, Herman Hesse.

I started with his book *Beneath the Wheel*. It's a criticism of the modern educational system. The main character, Hans, is a prodigy and the only kid from his village to ever get accepted at this prestigious seminary school. The first part of the book is the adults in the village vicariously living through him. There's the hypocritical pastor that teaches him Greek and Latin. Hans' father is rigid and strict which eventually leads to Hans' demise. I won't get too much more into it in case you want to read it someday. I can just say that I relate to Hans. He fell into the trap of conformity in modern society. Even though the book was written a long time ago it still resonates today. I knew I'd read everything by Hesse because San Antonio College isn't much of a challenge for me. The kids in most of my classes have IQ's of a fence post and are only there so they can transfer to the party university in the area, Texas State.

I had good grades at the end of the semester. I spent most of my time at the library and even started writing my thoughts down in a journal. I think Sanderson was right about expressing your feelings and writing for me seems to be the best way. I didn't think much about Sanderson anymore. I started to believe in myself and found enjoyment in learning. Those nerds back in high school knew what they were doing.

14

It sucks living at home but it's probably the best thing for now. Our Christmas break started, and I've always found Christmas depressing. It's like Easter because people don't give a damn about Jesus during the rest of the year. Everyone goes to the candlelight service and celebrates materialism the next day by opening presents. Don't get me wrong, there's nothing bad about it, but people forget about the real meaning of Christmas. That's especially true in my neighborhood, Alamo Heights. Everybody has money and is spoiled. I'm a bit of a hypocrite because I've always gotten what I want. To know the goddamn truth, I'm very blessed. My parents love and support me. I've made some mistakes but like Sanderson said, "That's part of life".

Growing up in the church, you kind of take it for granted. It becomes routine and after a while, you realize everyone is just there to get it over so they can go home and watch the Dallas Cowboys. Nothing worse than that team and they more than anything contributed to my hatred of sports. I disdain them because they symbolize all the fake patriotism and rallying around the flag.

I don't remember much about September 11th except for history books, but my parents talk about it sometimes. I've seen a bunch of videos on the internet about it and any rational person doesn't believe the government's official story. The sad thing is nobody questions anything. The bastards hauled off all the steel right away, so no real investigation could be done. Then everybody bowed down to the flag and praised the President for being our moral leader. The All-American crap they sell you on every time.

I'm doing better and trying not to think about the past. At night, sometimes my thoughts get the best of me and Amber always seems to be on my mind. She's in my dreams but not really in a sexual way. The violent ones are the worst, even if they come less and less now. Everybody has dreams, but it's the nightmares you always remember.

The Christmas break went by too fast. I'm still taking my basics plus a creative writing class and enjoying it. My professor is encouraging me to write a short story. I've already been writing my thoughts and a few poems in my journal, so it seemed only natural. When I wasn't in class, I started writing at home. My ideas seem to come best in my room and even though I've tried writing in Sam's room, something doesn't seem right. When I'm in there, it's like his ghost is watching over me. It's a creepy feeling. After a couple of times, I shut the door to Sam's room and didn't go in there anymore. I understand how my parents feel now, instead, and what Sanderson mentioned about "shared space." They still kind of deny he died, and by leaving his room alone, it's keeping him alive, but them away from it somehow, I don't know. I'll always remember him but also need to let him go. I'm not sure if heaven exists, but if there is one, Sam is there smiling down on me. That kind of makes everything seem alright for a while.

**

I came back from class one day and my Mom was sitting at the kitchen table crying.

"What's wrong?"

I had rarely seen my mother this hysterical. She didn't say anything but soon I saw why she was upset. The TV was on the local news and there had been a shooting at my high school.

I didn't believe it at first but soon the reality of it all came crashing down. I checked my phone and had tons of messages about it. There were several from Riley and Taylor and even Amber had texted me. I saw where my Dad had tried to call me, but I knew he was meeting with a client. I sat down and watched the news. They said a student walked into the cafeteria during lunch and opened fire. They weren't sure how many students had been killed or injured, but it was probably a lot. They couldn't ID the shooter just yet but they did confirm he committed suicide in the broom closet before the SWAT team came through. My mind became clouded and couldn't fathom what happened.

It didn't seem real, but nothing does until it affects you. I went into my room and started crying. The fact that I was in that cafeteria for four years, never thinking once how some crazy with a gun could pop in at any time and end my measly existence while I ate my BLT. Riley and Taylor would see my dead head drop into my tray and probably be the last thing they see before they get killed too. What a goddamn shit way to leave this planet and it just happened.

My Dad came home, and I heard him talking to my Mom. They were talking about me. My parents were concerned about how I was going to deal with this. He came by later and knocked on the door to my room. I didn't say anything and then he walked away. He probably knew I needed time to process everything. I went to the closet in my room and grabbed a bottle of vodka that I kept hidden. I took two of my pills and chugged about half of the bottle. I went to sleep with images of blood and dead bodies in my head. I began to blame myself. Hadn't I fantasized about doing this? It's like my nightmare had come true. I knew that I didn't do it but yet I felt responsible. The anxiety and intrusive thoughts began to overwhelm me.

**

When I woke up, I was in the hospital. At first, I didn't know if I was dreaming but then I noticed that I was hooked up to a heart monitor. A nurse came over and checked on me. She adjusted my bed and before she walked away, I said, "What happened?"

"Thank God you're conscious. You were in a coma and we had to pump your stomach. You're so lucky to be alive, young man. Somebody is looking out for you."

Those words didn't hit home right away, but later that night when I looked at the end of my bed, I saw Sam. He looked exactly like his last football portrait, pads and all. I had to shake my head over and over to get the image out, and then more nurses came by in a panic. I just heard a bunch of beeps like my heart was racing. All the time, he was smiling at me. I thought I died.

A week later, I was back home. I talked things out with my parents, and we decided that I needed professional help again. I went to Warm Springs which is the best rehab hospital in San Antonio. I tried to do the rest of my work inside, but at some point, my parents had to get me to sign a paper regarding a leave of absence.

**

After six weeks of treatment, I left the hospital. It wasn't long before Sanderson and I were talking again. This time I wanted to get better.

"Quite a maelstrom you've been in, Peyton," he said, flipping through the paperwork from the hospital and rehab.

"Yeah, I'd say," I said. My leg was twitching for a cigarette or a drink or sex maybe.

"So, did you know the kid that did the shooting?" Sanderson asked.

"I didn't know him, but I talked to him a few times. I tried being nice but knew he was being bullied. It seems strange but I knew James would do something like this."

"James?" Sanderson sat up in his chair and made a few notes.

"That's the kid that shot up the school. He was constantly being picked on by the jocks and popular kids. One time the principal caught him with a BB gun in his backpack. Why they let him back in school after that I'll never know. Alamo Heights is like that though. You know because James was Hispanic."

"What's that have to do with it?'

"You know Alamo Heights is almost all white, and the school district wants to be more diverse. Instead of kicking him out, they were more concerned about hurting him and his family's feelings. The district is going to get their ass sued off for that."

"Let's not go there. That's out of your control, Peyton." He was rigid in his chair now. "As far as your thoughts, do they make you feel guilty about it?"

"When it first happened, they did."

"I think your anxiety is certainly related to that, and sometimes when something tragic happens, it's easy to blame yourself. You're extremely fortunate to have your parents, you're very blessed."

"I know and I'm not going to take that for granted anymore."

"Or else, we wouldn't be talking right now," he said with a weird smile. "How do you feel about being out of school?"

"I never thought I would say this, but I miss it. I'll be ready to go back when I start feeling better."

"That's good to hear." He jogged the pages and looked at his watch. "Well, we're done for today. I'll see you next week. Be well."

Nine students died and a few others got injured. I didn't know any of them except one girl that was in my math class. What bothers me is that I keep thinking about that kid James. I should have talked to him more and tried to be his friend. High school is stupid and such a microcosm of our society. You have all the rich kid assholes at the top. All the popular kids that think their shit doesn't stink and then all the rejects at the bottom. Ironically, the rejects end up being much better people. Most of the popular kids never amount to anything and end up resting on the laurels of their rich bastard parents. Nobody did the one thing that would have mattered the most to James. Nobody listened to him.

Amber didn't seem all that important to me anymore. I spent so much time obsessing over her, and now we never talked. Sanderson was right about being too young to fall in love. You don't want to get stuck on one girl too soon. Even Sam told me this when I was a kid. He was a real lady's man. For the first time in a while, I felt optimistic about life.

**

"So, do you think you've had time to process things?" Sanderson asked.

"I think so and I'm getting back into skating again. That's making me feel better, plus I stopped drinking."

"How do you feel about that Peyton?"

"I feel a lot better physically and my mind is in a better place. I know it's not easy. They told me that in rehab. You know, that one day at a time mantra."

"Mantra? Aren't you a little philosopher now?" Sanderson laughed.

"I'm reading more too and looking forward to getting back in school. I think I'm being more honest with myself."

"That's great, Peyton. No need to get down on yourself. You have a lot going on for yourself. Stay on your medication and let me know if you need anything. Tell your folks I said hello."

I walked out of Sanderson's office. I decided to skate to my appointment because the weather was nice. Soon, it would be summer and hotter than hell. The heat is the worst thing about San Antonio besides the Alamo. It's hard to believe that this all started when I skipped my high school graduation. I should have walked across that stage with my friends instead of running away from myself. I laughed thinking about how stupid the whole thing had been. I showed off some tricks in front of some young teens. They cheered for me and I winked.

When I got home, I decided to go for a walk. I walked over to the park and then I saw her. Amber.

"I didn't know you were home," I said.

"Oh, hi, stranger. I'm home for a week or so. How have you been?" Amber asked.

"I'm doing better, thanks for asking."

"Listen, I've been thinking about things. I love you, Peyton. I want to be with you. I realize that now."

I didn't know what to say. I hugged her and then I walked away with a smile. I suppose I could tell you what happened after that, but then we'd get nowhere fast.

ABOUT THE AUTHOR

Thom Young is a writer from Texas. His work has been in *PBS Newshour, The Wall Street Journal, F(r)iction, The Oxford Review*, and over a hundred literary journals, as well as two poetry collections and four novels. He won a 2008 Million Writers Award and a nomination for the 2016 Pushcart Prize. You can follow him @tyypoet on Instagram.

www.ingramcontent.com/pod-product-compliance
Lightning Source LLC
Chambersburg PA
CBHW020253130626
46549CB00005B/2202